Prologue

"He's out of control" Vincent hissed to his son – making sure he kept his voice quiet. The room wasn't soundproof, and they were worried that people would hear them.

"What do we do, Sir?" Saxon whispered, voice as urgent as his fathers. "We can't overthrow him. He's the Alpha". Saxon looked at his father, noticing the way he was aging – the grey wisps in his hair, the wrinkles that were growing under his eyes and his forehead.

"We can, but we have to do it politically. There will be none of this old fashioned fighting and killing like barbarians. This will be done properly and with the right course of action. But, I need to meet the criteria to take over as Alpha".

Saxon nodded, "we need to make your Pack larger and stronger".

Vincent smiled at his youngest son, "exactly. Your brothers and I need to stay here with the Alpha, and the rest of the Council. It will look suspicious if we suddenly all up and leave during a Council meeting. But, listen, if we do this, we do it properly. There will be no Forced Turns, do you understand?"

"Understood Sir" Saxon smiled, glancing at his watch. "How long do I have?"

"One month" Vincent replied. "You have one month to get as many Pack members as you can. But none can be a Forced Turn. Because we'll be able to smell it in their scents if you Force Turn anyone, Saxon".

"I would never do that, Sir" he frowned, slightly offended by his father's distrust.

"I know you wouldn't Saxon. But you have to understand that it will be a frustrating month, when most of your chosen people are failing the change. You're a compassionate boy, Saxon, you get it from your mother. So I know you would never Force a change on purpose, but when you see someone dying, it's very hard to turn away".

"I know what I have to do, father. We cannot allow the Alpha to carry on like this" Saxon nodded. Vincent nodded at his son, pride flowing through him, before he clasped his shoulder firmly.

"Go, son, go build our Pack up again". Vincent gave his youngest son a quick hug, before heading out the door. Saxon stared at the closed door for a moment, knowing his father had tasked him with an important job.

Saxon had six older brothers, and spent his life in the shadow of them all. Yet, finally, his father had trusted him with a big task – to make their Pack the strongest, so that his father could take over as the Alpha.

So, Saxon quickly packed a bag and headed to the airport. He had a hard task ahead of him, but he was excited to get started.

Chapter One

Frowning, I curled my hands into fists at my sides. I couldn't believe him, I couldn't *fucking* believe him. When I got my hands on him, I was going rip him a new one. I had never been so angry in my entire life.

Getting out of my car, I gave the front tyre a kick in anger. First he cheated on me, then he didn't even have the decency to put fuel in his car. Granted, I had stolen the car, but still, he should have filled it up.

It was dark out, and I wasn't really sure where I was. I didn't have many thoughts when I came home; found my boyfriend screwing his ex-girlfriend, punched the bastard in the face, stole his car, and drove into the night.

So there I was, standing in the middle of nowhere, with a car out of gas when suddenly a car pulled up behind me. Two men stepped out. Now, I probably should have run the other way, and got the hell out of there. That would have been the responsible thing to do. But, then, I never said I was responsible.

"You alright there?" one of them asked. I frowned, eyeing them both up and down. They were both tall, with swept back black hair, and dark eyes. There was no denying they were brothers, but I couldn't work out which was older. They didn't seem overly suspicious, but I knew from experience that stranger danger was a real thing.

"I'm out of gas" I replied, glancing back into the car – where I knew there was a 9mm in the glove compartment. I had no idea how to shot a gun; I was British, but I was pretty sure I could work it out.

"That's a beautiful accent you have there" the shorter of the brother's smiled, eyes shining in the night. Even though we were just outside Toronto, his accent sounded like it was from Louisiana.

"You got any gas in your truck?" I asked, nodding to the pick-up they had gotten out of. The brothers exchanged looks. I frowned, a bad feeling creeping up my spine. I was pretty sure whatever those men wanted, it wasn't helping a women in need.

"I don't know, Travis, have we got some gas?" the shorter one questioned his brother, smirking like they knew something I didn't.

"One second, beautiful, let me just check" Travis smiled slyly, before walking back to their truck. I glanced at my car, wondering if I should dive in and get that gun. But I didn't have chance, as the other brother moved closer to me.

"So you got a name, beautiful?" the other brother asked, leaning against my car – his arm against my door so I wouldn't get to open it.

"Of course I have name" I rolled my eyes. His jaw clenched, and I could tell he didn't like my attitude – because I did have a bad attitude. But, he kept his bright grin up. "Jessica" I lied, not wanting to tell him my real name.

"A beautiful girl, with a beautiful name and a beautiful accent" he purred, eyes looking me up and down. I pouted my lips, glancing around. Thick forestry surrounded us, and I knew that I would be screwed if everything went south – which with the spine crawling feeling I had, I was pretty sure it would.

"Sorry Miles, looks like we've used the last of the gas" Travis smiled, walking back towards us. "We'll just have to give you a ride, beautiful".

"I'm waiting for a tow truck" I replied, automatically taking a step back. The brothers exchanged a look – and my blood ran cold.

"Come on now Jessica" Miles smiled, moving closer to me. I stepped back again, as Travis rushed forward and grabbed my arm. I fought against his hold, but he just held on tighter. Miles jumped forward, and grabbed my other arm when he noticed my fight.

"Let me go" I spat, as they both pressed me up against my car.

"Look Jessica, we can do this the hard way or the easy way" Travis smiled, as his brother pressed his large body to mine.

"Where did you get that line? Handbook of asshole's clichés?" I growled at them, still trying to push past them but to no avail. The brothers laughed warmly, but it was a bitter and twisted laugh. Miles pushed up against me, his body crushing mine as his beer soaked breath fanned over my neck. "Fuck you" I spat.

"Oh but we'd much rather fuck you" he whispered huskily, and I felt him press his erection into my leg – the hardness obvious even with his thick jeans. Sickness plagued my stomach, and I tried to push him off, but nothing happened.

Travis let out a booming laugh, "oh she a fighter. I love it when they're feisty". He licked his lips, and the bile in my throat threatened to escape. Miles licked my neck, and I shivered in disgust. "Come on, Miles, we should get her in the truck just in case someone drives past".

Miles groaned in complaint, but moved his head out of my neck. He pulled away, but with his body still pressed to mine. "Travis grab the rope, I think she's going to be a fighter" Miles smirked down at me. Travis laughed, as his brother groped my chest.

Pulling back slightly, I spat straight into Miles's face. His face went from entertained to furious in a millisecond. Pulling back, he grabbed my hand and pulled me towards his truck. Knowing I had to escape, I pulled at the last bit of courage I had.

Pulling my foot back, I whipped it forward and kicked Miles straight in the crotch. He yelped in pain, and his grip loosen enough for me to pull free. As he grabbed at his – soon to be – bruised balls, I took off sprinting.

Both Miles and Travis shouted after me, as I ran into the forest. I wasn't quiet as I ran, my feet crunching every leaf and every twig, and my shirt catching on every tree I passed. I was breathing heavily, as I fought through the darkness.

I ran for a few minutes, before a bullet zipped past my left. I screamed in shock, and hit the floor. "That way" I heard Travis shout, at the same time I heard the reload of a shotgun. I cussed mentally, as I crawled through the forest.

I wanted to get up and run, but I didn't want to be shot at. So I kept to my army crawl, my arms and core muscles screaming in pain. As I heard Travis and Miles gaining on me, I pulled myself under a bush.

I curled up into myself, as I tried to make myself as small as possible. Sweat poured down my face, as my heart thumped wildly. "Come on out bitch" Miles growled, mere meters away from where I was hidden. I pressed my hand over my mouth – to silence my heavy breathing.

"Miles let's just leave it. Let the bitch die out here" Travis sighed, annoyed. I willed for Miles to agree with his brother. But I was all out of luck.

"I'm not letting that bitch get away with that. I am going to fuck her until she's raw and begging me to stop. And then I'm going to fuck her some more and then leave her out here to die" he growled back. I gulped at the visual his words painted.

The forest rustled close, and I assumed it was them. "What was that?" Travis demanded.

"That's a fucking dead bitch is what that is" Miles replied, and there footsteps grew closer. Moving out from the bush, I knew if I didn't run they would soon be on top of me. Gun or no gun, I had to run.

I tripped to my feet, before taking off. I sprinted through the trees. "Over there" one of the brother screamed, and soon they were right behind me. "Don't shoot her" Miles ordered his brother, "I want to hear this bitch scream".

And then, because I had more bad luck – than someone who smashed a mirror while walking under a ladder with a black cat – I tripped. I went flying into the floor, scrapping across the ground. In a second, Miles and Travis were on me.

With a large shotgun pointed at me, the brothers came to a stop. They both shared a sadistic smile, as they loomed over me. I didn't dare move, although I wanted to fight with every aspect of my body.

"Oh I am going to enjoy this" Miles growled out, that terrifying smile burning itself into my memory so that it would appear in my nightmares later. He reached down and grabbed my arm, his grip hurt me as he haled me to my feet.

I yelped in pain, as he pushed me against the trunk of a tree. As Miles got into my face, a rustling started in the bushes next to us. "What the hell is that?" Travis asked, the barrel of his gun swinging around frantically.

"It'll just be a rabbit or something. Shut up and let's finish this" Miles growled, before he slammed his lips onto mine. I fought against the kiss, as his teeth bit my lips and drew blood. I whimpered in pain, as his hands slammed my back into the trunk again.

Then, a loud roar sounded to our left. We all froze – paralysed in fear for the creature that could have created such a noise. "What was that?" Miles asked, pulling his body away from me; but his hands still gripping me in position.

Miles's question was answered by a large, midnight black, Wolf diving from the bushes. The Wolf was large, and muscled, his muzzled covered in blood from its previous hunts. The darkness of his fur made him almost undetectable in the night, but I was sure with his large eyes he had no problem seeing his next meals.

Travis cussed, and raised his gun. But before his finger was even positioned to pull the trigger, the Wolf lunged. His large form hit Travis, and the two of them fell to the floor. Miles yelped in shock, as blood splattered over the two of us.

With me forgotten, Miles took off into the night. He didn't even get ten meters, before the Wolf turned away from Travis' corpse and went after Miles. He was on him within seconds. I didn't particularly like either man, but I cringed at their bloody deaths.

The Wolf's muzzle sunk into Miles's neck, ripping his jugular out and causing scarlet liquid to cover the beast's large pearly white teeth. I gulped deeply, knowing I would be next. I shuffled slightly, my foot snagging on a twig. The noise made the Wolf turned to me.

"Nice doggy, good doggy" I muttered, holding my hands out in a surrender gesture. The Wolf looked at me, head cocking as if studying me. "Yes, nice doggy. You enjoy your meal and just let me go". My words made the Wolf cock his head to the other side. Then, the Wolf let out a snort – which I swore was a laugh.

I backed up a step, testing the water, and the Wolf growled. I froze instantly, heart pounding. "Alright, I'm not going anywhere. Why don't you get back to your meal?" I swallowed deeply, having no idea why I was speaking to a Wolf who had no idea what I was saying.

The Wolf studied me for a second, before he took a step towards me. "Fuck" I whispered, and the Wolf made another snorting noise. I tried to move back again, but he growled – he didn't like that. But, I was damned if I was going to be; cheated on, groped, chased, shot at *and* eaten all in one day. So I took off running.

It was useless. The Wolf howled in annoyance, and then he was on me.

Chapter Two

I woke up in an unknown bedroom. I freaked out – having no idea how I got there and or where 'there' was. "Easy, easy" a male voice called out. I was laying on a bed, in a dodgy looking cabin – with only the natural light from the window streaming in.

I was still wearing my jeans, and my shirt, but both were ripped which I was sure they weren't before – even with the rape-y brother's grabby hands. My head was pounding, and my chest hurt, but the majority of my pain came from my hip.

At the sound of the male voice, my head whipped around the room. I quickly found the source of the voice. A tall man, with a large muscled body, sat in a chair against the far wall. He had jet back hair, which was swept back with natural perspiration, and his face was harsh and chiselled.

He was attractive – but at that moment, his beauty was the last thing on my mind.

"Where am I?" I demanded, as he moved closer. As he stepped into the sunlight, I noticed the rest of his beauty; ivory white skin, sharp jaw, shiny white teeth, dimples on each cheek and eyes dark but with speckled gold in them.

"You're safe, I promise" he held his hands up softly. His voice was smooth, and had a royal strength to it. "You've been hurt. But you're safe".

"The Wolf" I gasped, and a small smile stretched onto his face. "What happened to the Wolf? And those guys he killed? I can't remember anything past me hitting the floor".

The man nodded, "you knocked your head. You went unconscious immediately". He took a seat on the edge of the bed, and I scooted away a few inches. I glared at him in distrust, but he didn't seem offended. "These are from Wolf claws" he pointed to my ripped jeans, "you were dragged back here".

"Why didn't the Wolf eat me?" I questioned.

"That Wolf was saving you, not hurting you" he told me, his eyes watching me closely. Reaching forward, he took a hold of the hem of my shirt. I pushed his hands off me, and scooted away again. His hands shot into a surrender gesture. "I heard what those guys tried to do. I wasn't trying anything, I was just showing you your injuries".

I didn't say anything, I just pulled my shirt up myself. A large white bandage was over my right hip, which was where most of my pain came from. "You were bitten" he exclaimed, "that's why you feel so bad".

"Sorry, who are you?" I questioned, raising my eyebrows in annoyance.

"My name is Saxon. I was out in the forest, I heard you scream" he explained, and I frowned. "I heard them call you Jessica. Is that your name?"

"No. My name is Chelsea" I replied. "How did you scare the Wolf off?" I wasn't convinced by his 'hero' routine.

"I told you, Chelsea, the Wolf wasn't trying to hurt you. The Wolf saved your life. He never wanted to hurt you. He only pounced because you tried to run. It's instinct to chase something that runs. That was all that happened. The Wolf didn't mean to hurt you".

"How do you know? Do you speak Wolf?" I crossed my arms tightly under my chest. Saxon's eyes darted down to my cleavage, before his eyes popped back to mine.

"I don't speak Wolf, Chelsea. I was that Wolf" he told me, completely serious. "Do you want some water?"

"Wait. No, hold on a second. You can't just claim to be half Wolf, and then offer me a drink. Explain, explain". I was getting hysterical – wondering just *how* hard I had hit my head.

"I was born to a human mother, and a Werewolf father. On my eighteen birthday I shifted into a Wolf for the first time, just as all my brothers had. Now, it is my job to repopulate my Pack with fresh Wolves. You are my first new Pack member. Now, I really think you should have some water".

"Fine, water, yes. But first go back to all the crazy Wolf Pack shit you were talking about" I urged, wondering where the hell they let Saxon out of. He didn't answer, he simply got up and headed out the bedroom. The dark cabin groaned as he walked through.

I got up and followed him – my hip throbbing in pain. I hissed as I reached the doorway, hand instantly going to where the Wolf, who apparently was also Saxon, had bitten me. I yelped in pain, as I rested against the frame.

"Shit, Chelsea" Saxon cussed, in front of me quicker than humanly possible. His large, callous, hands went around me instantly. He held me with strength, before leading me over to an old tattered couch. As I sat down, cringing in pain, I glanced around the cabin.

It was old fashioned, and full of dust and grime. I was shocked it even had running water, but when I noticed the bottle in Saxon's hand I realised it didn't. "Do you live here?"

"No I just brought you here last night, because I couldn't dress your wounds in my car" Saxon told me, sitting down next to me and handing me the bottled water. "I only stopped here for a run".

"A run. Right, because you're a Werewolf right?" I said slowly. Saxon gave me a look.

"Yes, because I'm a Werewolf". He still didn't look like he was joking, and I was getting worried he thought he was actually some sort of shape shifter.

"Alright if you are a Werewolf, like you say you are, then isn't there some kind of Wolf law against telling humans against what you are?" I questioned, playing along because I wanted to escape at some point.

His lips quivered for a moment. "Yes there are rules, but there are exceptions. Like with the fact that I bit you".

"Ah, so now I'm going to turn into a Werewolf too, right?"

Saxon sighed, "you don't believe me?"

"Would you believe you?" I gave him a look, and he breathed out a laugh before running his hands down his face.

"Alright fine, I'll show you. Just don't scream, my ears are very sensitive" he grumbled, before pulling his shirt off. For a moment I shamelessly checked him out, incredibly pleased with what I saw, before I realised there was a complete stranger standing in front of me removing his clothing.

I wasn't really sure what to do, when he was finally naked and knelt down on all fours. Hundreds of jokes ran though my head, but I kept them to myself. Saxon let out a groan, I bit my lip to stop my laughter.

But then, Saxon's body began to morph. "No fucking way" I breathed out, eyes watching Saxon's form in shock and fascination. His back arched up; the rigid sections of his spine obvious through his milky skin.

His arms and legs began to extend, and awful cracking sound ringing through the small cabin. Saxon then looked up at me, his dark eyes widening and his nose and mouth stretching out into a muzzle shape.

I gulped, as dark hair began to sprout over his body – the natural dark hair on the top of his head, growing and extending over his face and back. His back arched and Saxon made a noise of pain, as his head folded in as his body carried on growing.

Then, seconds later, there was nothing of Saxon left. Well, not the Saxon I had just met. Standing in front of me – well more like *looming* in front of me – was the same Wolf that had saved me the night before. "Holy fucking shit balls" I swore, having nothing else to say.

Saxon made a noise, a snorting sort of laugh. "You can understand me right?" I asked, and he nodded his head. "Did that hurt?" I asked, he nodded yes then shook his head no. "Yes and no?" I laughed, and he huffed. "Sometimes?" I tried, and he nodded yes. "So sometimes it hurts".

I stared at him for a moment, having no idea what the hell to say. "Will I be able to that too?" I asked, and he nodded yes. I let out another string of colourful cusses, and I leaned back against the ancient couch in shock.

I had a very mundane life before, and suddenly I had been thrust into a world of crazy and unbelievable. Saxon, who was a Werewolf, had bitten me, thus turning me into a Werewolf. I would soon have the ability to turn into a Wolf, like Saxon could.

Of course I was scared, and terrified by that. Yet, at the same time, a deep rooted excited was pitted in my stomach. I wanted to be able to change form, I wanted to be a predator, and I wanted to be a Werewolf.

Why wouldn't I? I had a quiet, mundane, life with no strong ties to anyone. I could imagine nothing more exciting than having a new life – one full of secrets, and excitement and strength. I was scared, no doubt about it, but at the same time I was eager.

As I thought everything over, Saxon shifted back. I watched for a few seconds, before going back to my thoughts. "Should I feel upset?" I asked Saxon, as he redressed.

"I don't know. Everyone feels different about it. How do you feel?"

"Excited" I replied, and a small smile edged onto his features. "I always say I want to be a different person, in a different life, in a different body. And, now, you've offered me that" I grinned.

Saxon took a sit next to me, hands taking mine. Usually, I hated people invading my personal space but with Saxon I didn't mind too much. "So can I do that? Change into a Wolf?" I asked.

He shook his head negatively, "you've only gotten through the first part of the transition. You've still got a long way to go until you'll be a Werewolf".

Chapter Three

"Explain it to me" I asked Saxon, "please explain everything".

"Right. So, there are about two thousand Werewolves worldwide. We're a small race, and we are all under the rule of an Alpha. Each Wolf Pack is run by a Dominant, and these Dominants work directly under the Alpha. There is only one Alpha in the entire world. He sets the rules, he gives orders, and no one can disobey him".

"Do you vote for an Alpha?"

"Yes, but the once the Alpha is in place his reign will carry on until his death. Except in extreme situations, in which there are lots of political roots to be taken. But I won't bore you with politics at the moment". Saxon paused, looking deep in thought, before carrying on.

"I was born a Werewolf, but you can also be made into one through getting saliva into the bloodstream. Like how I bit you. However, only a Werewolf that is born can make a Werewolf. You couldn't bite a human and change them" he explained, and I nodded in understanding.

"When you're bitten, there is two parts to the change. First, surviving the initial bite – which you have. That's a good sign, because most people will take an allergic reaction to the bite, and will go into anaphylactic shock. It's very rare that doesn't happen. As in one in ten".

"So there was a one in ten chance I would be dead right now?" I frowned, not liking that he had gambled with my life.

"No there was about a one in a hundred chance you would have been died" Saxon admitted truthfully. "Female Wolves are very, very rare. I have only ever met two in my life, because they can't be born. A male Werewolf can only bare male children, so She Wolves can only be made. And they hardly ever survive".

"I guess you're pretty shocked I survived then" I commented bluntly, crossing my arms again. I was showing Saxon how unhappy I was with him playing Russian roulette with my life. He gave a small shrug.

"Yeah. I would have put my money on you not surviving the night".

"I'm a stubborn bitch when I need to be" I replied, and he huffed out a laugh.

"I can see that. Anyway, like I said, there are two stages to the initial shift. First, survive the bite. And secondly, survive the fever". He looked at me seriously for a moment, his hands still clasped around mine. There was a hardness to his eyes.

"What's the fever?" I asked nervously.

"You'll find out soon enough. But, the problem is that I can get you through the fever by biting you again. But I can't do that. Forcing your shift, is not only illegal, but would mean that if the Alpha found you he would kill you. Only Forced Turns that have proven themselves to the Alpha are allowed to live. A Wolf that had a Forced Turn is highly dangerous. They can never control themselves, and they have violent outbursts and large bloodlust."

"So I have to get myself through the fever?" I gulped, and Saxon nodded. "When will the fever hit?"

"I'm surprised it hasn't hit already" he replied, giving my hands a squeeze. "Chelsea, I didn't bite you just because I felt the urge to. I did it, because I am building up my Pack. The more Wolves, the stronger the Pack. The Alpha is getting out of control, abusing his position, and my father wants to overthrow him. But, one of the rules to strip an Alpha of his positon, is that the next to take charge, my father, has to have the strongest and largest Pack".

"So you're stock piling Werewolves".

"Kind of. I do have to say though, if we were to have a She Wolf our Pack would instantly shoot up in strength. So, no pressure, but please survive the fever. It would really help me out. And, well, I want you to survive. I like you Chelsea, you'll be my first Turn, and I'll be your Sire".

After a while of talking, Saxon led me out to his car and we drove to his apartment in Toronto. "You're sure you don't want to go back for your car?" he asked, as we twisted through the roads.

"I stole it anyway" I shrugged, and he snapped his head to me. "Only from my ex-boyfriend. Caught the bastard cheating on me, so I gave him a black eye and stole his car". There was a moment of slapstick style surprise from him, before Saxon chuckled and shook his head.

"You'll survive the fever just fine". He shook his head, amused by my actions. Saxon explained to me that even though he was building up his Pack, he hadn't meant to turn anyone in Toronto – because that was where his home was.

However, when he had returned home to pack a bag, he decided to take one last run in the forest he knew better than any other. And when he heard me, he knew he couldn't let the men get away with raping me. So he'd come to save me – and then in the spare of the moment bitten me.

His apartment, in downtown Toronto, was large and modern. We headed inside, and I was shocked with how nice it was. "What do you do?" I asked, gaping slightly.

"I'm a PI" he replied, and I smiled. "I got into it so that I can watch over the crimes associated with Werewolves, and make sure no one gets their noses too deep into it. But most of the cases I take are completely human".

"Lots of travelling then. It sounds fun, I wish I could do something like that. I barely make my rent most months". I glanced over the expensive furniture, and I couldn't deny that I was slightly jealous.

"What do you do?" Saxon asked, I could feel his eyes on me as I walked over to the French doors and glanced out at the balcony.

"I'm a stripper" I replied, and I had a feeling Saxon almost choked on his own spit. "Yeah, can't say I'm exactly proud of it. But I don't exactly have many job opportunities". There was a soft blush on his face – in Saxon's world, not many people were strippers and he didn't know what to say to me. I turned away from him.

A hand touched my back, and I jumped slightly. "You've got your whole life ahead of you, Chelsea. Once you get through the fever, you can be whatever you want to be". Saxon's breath was right behind me, and I couldn't help but smile sadly.

"Let's just get through the fever first" I nodded, as Saxon's hand slipped away from my back. "Have you got any food? I'm hungry?"

Saxon and I ate together at his kitchen table, Saxon answering all the questions I had – and there were lots of them. He explained about the way to Turn into a Werewolf, about his life, his Pack, his Dominant.

"So if you're my Sire, does that mean that I am owned by you?" I questioned, as Saxon placed our dirty plates in the sink.

"Not owed no. But we'll have a deep rooted connection. You'll see me as someone to look up, someone to respect. You'll see me like a teacher to you" he explained, before pouring me another glass of water. He paused, looking at me. "You haven't asked about the fever yet".

"I'd rather not know. It's doesn't exactly sound pleasant. So I'd rather go into it not knowing" I gave a shrug. Saxon studied me for a moment, before nodding but his eyes didn't look like they understood. I had a feeling that Saxon was one of those people who needed to know everything – he didn't like being left in the dark. I, on the other hand, didn't mind being in the dark, as long as the things in the dark didn't bite.

"How are you feeling?" Saxon asked, stepping next to me and placing his hand on my forehead. "You look like you're building a sweat up".

"I feel fine" I replied, looking up into Saxon's face. He frowned, biting my lip, as his eyebrows burrowed downwards. He looked very concerned, and I couldn't help but admire how attractive he was from that angle – well, from any angle really.

"You feel warm. I think the fever might be starting".

"How long does it last?"

"I have no idea. You're my first Turn remember?" His frowned deeper. "Why don't you go and take a cold shower? Better to catch the heat early, while we have chance to contain it".

I agreed, and he walked me through his bedroom and to his bathroom. He left me with a set of clean towels, and one of his shirts to change into. I thanked him, and stepped into the shower. Once he mentioned it, I did feel a bit sweaty.

So I made sure the shower was cold, as I washed my bruised body. I took the dressing off my bite wound, cringing as I did so. The bite itself was obvious – red, bloody, teeth marks on my hip. As soon as the water touched it, it began to bleed once more. However, I could see it was beginning to scab.

I washed the rest of my body, the water darkening from all the mud and forest filth that was rinsed off my body. The water seemed to keep getting hotter, so I kept turning it colder and colder, until it couldn't get any colder. It was then I realised the water wasn't getting hotter, I was just burning up. The water was no longer doing anything, so I turned it off.

I let out a heavy breath, as I opened the shower doors. Cold air hit my wet body, and momentarily the heat dried up. Then as quickly as it left, the heat came back again. I cussed, my head going dizzy for a moment.

"Chelsea" Saxon's voice was right outside the bathroom door. "Are you alright?"

"It's starting" I breathed out, collapsing to all fours. He opened the door, breaking the lock as he did so. I didn't even care I was naked, and neither did he. Saxon knelt in front of me, hands pushing my wet hair away from my face.

Saxon looked at me with fear in his eyes, as the room span and my body sweated from every crevice I had. Saxon took a deep breath, before moving away from me and walking over to the bath. He turned the dial to freezing, and let the water run out the taps.

I stayed on the floor, sitting back so my back was against the shower door. The room carried on spinning, and I felt tears prickle in my eyes. I didn't ever cry, but I was so hot that I began to cry. I didn't sob, just rogue tears that escaped my ducts ran down my face.

Saxon returned with a bucket of ice, and emptied it into the bath. As he let the water fill the rest of the tub, he turned the air-con dial on the doorway – cold air filled the room. It felt nice against my hot body, but I was still too hot to even order my thoughts.

"Saxon" I breathed out. "I think I'm going to die".

"No you're not, Chelsea" Saxon growled out, determination in his voice. "You can fight this, I know you can. Promise me you'll fight this". When I didn't reply, he repeated the word again. "Promise me".

"I promise" I finally breathed out, before the delirium slipped in.

Chapter Four

Saxon pulled me to my feet, but my body had given up its motor function, so I just collapsed again. Saxon muttered an oath, before catching me before I hit the floor. Without so much as a groan, he picked me up bridal style.

He slipped me into the ice bath, and I moaned with how nice it felt. Saxon slipped my naked body all the way inside the tub, before letting me go. I closed my eyes, enjoying the sensation for a moment. I jumped a mile when I felt something touch me.

"Easy there" Saxon breathed out, crouching down next to the bath. His eyes looked into mine, as he knelt down, holding an ice pack to my forehead. I offered him a small smile, as my eyes closed again. He held the ice pack to my head, and for a moment I just listened to his steady breathing.

Colours flew and dipped in front of my eyes, whisking around each other wildly. It was pretty, and for a moment I watched the swirling colours. Then, the colours began to change – morphing into people. I gasped when I saw my mother's face in front of me; the colours all wrong and her face looking like it was made up of smoke.

"Chelsea?" she questioned, in a voice that didn't belong to her. I groaned, not being able to speak. "Chelsea, come back to me. It's Saxon" my mother said. I was confused for a long while, wondering who Saxon was and why my mother was speaking in a male voice. "Shit, your heart is slowing down" my mother said. My mother never cussed.

I wondered why my heart was slowing down, and then I remembered that it was because of the heat. And then I remembered the heat was part of the fever, and the fever was from the bite Saxon had given me.

"Saxon?" I groaned, my mother disappearing into colours again.

"Chelsea, hey, open your eyes. I'm here" Saxon replied, but the problem was that I didn't know how to open my eyes – because I couldn't work out where my eyes were. Taking a deep breath, I tried to picture my eyes in my mind.

They were a bright turquoise, with a thick black line around them. My eyes looked like they were green, but then I had covered them with blue contacts. In the light they shone a blue sapphire, and in the dark they looked like a neon green. I were told they were beautiful eyes, and I tried to recall them in my mind.

I pictured myself in front of a mirror, looking into my eyes. In the mental image, I closed my eyes before slowly opening them. Light filled my mind for a moment, before darkness came back. I was getting there. I pictured it again, slowly closing and then reopening my eyes. The second time, my eyes did open.

Everything was bright for a while, and I groaned, as my eyes adjusted to the brightness. But still everything was too light for me to see anything. "Chelsea, are you alright?"

"Too bright" I complained. I didn't want to close my eyes again, scared I would not be able to reopen them. So I simply placed my hand over my eyes; blocking as much light as I could.

"Don't close your eyes" Saxon insisted, before I heard movement. Seconds later he was placing something on my eyes. Sunglasses I quickly realised, as I moved my hands away. The dark lenses blocked enough light out that I was able to keep my eyes open. I glanced at Saxon, who was crouched at the side of the bath.

"How long was I out of it?"

"About forty minutes. It scared me, I thought you were a goner for a while there". He gave me a nervous smile, and I could see the wetness of his sleeves. No doubt he had to keep pulling me up so I didn't slip under the water.

I was shocked I had been dreaming of those colours for so long, it felt like a matter of seconds to me. I looked at Saxon for a moment, before I saw movement behind him. He saw my eye movement, and glanced behind him. "Chelsea focus on me, alright?"

But I couldn't, because light was growing behind him. The swirl of colours returning in a large moving circle behind him – a whirlwind of colour and light. And it was sucking me in. I screamed as I began to fall into the colour; flying through the bathroom and into the sink hole.

Colours surrounded my body; filling my mouth, and my nose and my eyes. I choked, and suffocated on the colours. I tried to screamed, and fight, but nothing was happening. I was being killed by colours – they were choking me, burning me, drowning me.

Then I took a big breath, and I was back in the bathroom. Saxon was in front of me, hands holding me as I coughed and choked, and tried to get air back into my lungs. "Deep breath" Saxon told me, as his arms held me slightly out of the water.

I then realised that I hadn't been drowning in colour, I had been drowning in water. When I was calmed down enough, to breathe normally, Saxon set me back down in the tub. I groaned – chest hurting from all the water I'd obviously taken in – as I rested my head against the rim.

"Sunglasses" I croaked out, as the light began to hurt my eyes again. Saxon nodded, hands dipping into the water, as he pulled the glasses that had gone under. He then placed them on my face once more. I took a deep breath, coughing again.

"Chelsea, you're doing really well. And I'm right here, I promise" Saxon said, pushing my dark hair out of my face once more. I nodded, not convinced as I felt a stirring in my stomach.

"Saxon" I groaned, and he made a noise telling me to continue. "Saxon, I'm going to be sick" I breathed out, right before my body convulsed and I violently threw up over the edge of the bath. The majority of it hit Saxon, who cussed, as the bile burnt its way out of my throat.

I tried to take a deep breath, but my nose was blocked and my throat was burning with the vomit that flew from it. I couldn't breathe, and the bile just kept flowing from my mouth. Saxon, still damp from the water and covered in my puke, held the ice bowl in front of me and rubbed my back.

When I finally emptied my stomach, I managed to take a deep breath as my body shook violently. "Sorry" I stuttered out, my entire body beginning to shake wildly.

"You have nothing to apologise for, Chelsea" Saxon replied, offering me a small smile looking nothing but worried. "Are you cold?" he asked, noticing my shaking.

"No. Pain" I whispered, as I glanced my shaking legs. I whimpered when I noticed my skin moving, as if there was something under the skin trying to get out. And then pain erupted in my leg, as the skin ripped open and a dark beetle looking bug burst out from my skin.

I screamed, as I noticed other bugs moving under my skin. I began to hit them, hoping to kill them before they could burst from my skin. I screamed, and shouted, as none of them would die. They just crawled under my skin, no matter how many times I hit myself.

Large arms lifted me up, when I realised I had slipped under the water in my fight with the bugs. I carried on screaming, and trying to break out of the arm's grips. I needed to kill those bugs before they broke out of my skin.

But the strong grip held me down, and one by one bugs began to break from my skin. I screamed, and I cried, and I screamed as bugs burst from my skin – causing blood to explode from my arms, my legs and the rest of my body. I thrashed as the water turned red from blood, as the bugs swam inside it.

"Chelsea calm down" Saxon's voice called out to me. I snapped my eyes up to his face, to see the strain in his expression as he held me down. I took a breath, before looking back at the water. It was no longer red, and there were no bugs, and my body was completely fine. I let a deep breath out.

I let out a deep cuss, as Saxon found the sunglasses once more. "No, I'm fine, I'm fine" I told him, batting the glasses from his hand. He nodded, before slowly releasing my arms when he realised I was done fighting to kill those imaginary bugs under my skin.

I stayed staring at Saxon for a good five minutes, and he just watched me – both of us breathing hard. "I think it's over" I whispered, hoping I wasn't jinxing anything. Saxon nodded, a small smile slipping on his lips.

"You've done it" he grinned manically, "you survived the fever. I was scared, your heart stopped a few times. But it started itself up every time. And your pulse was so low, it was scary. But your heart beat sounds strong now, and you don't look like you're about to pass out".

"Will you help me out?" I asked, raising my arms. I was exhausted and the idea of even standing was like running up the side of Everest. Saxon took hold of me, and lifted me out the tub. He dodged past the mess of the bathroom, and walked me into the bedroom. He set me down on the bed.

"I'm really tired" I whispered, as Saxon moved away and began to remove his filthy clothing.

"Go to sleep" he told me, as my eyes began to flutter. I nodded, the last thing I saw was his shirt being discarded into the bin.

It felt like I had just closed my eyes, when I woke up. I had the worse cramp in my leg, and I yelled out in pain – unable to move my legs. Saxon was at my bed side in a matter of second – showered, dressed and ready for action.

Another cramp shot through my other leg, and I buckled in pain. Saxon ripped the blanket off me, his eyes flittering down to my thighs. "You're Shifting" he informed me smiling.

Chapter Five

Saxon lifted me up, and placed me on the bedroom floor. With incredible strength, he pushed the bed to the other side of the room – leaving the large part of the floor bare. Saxon was back in front of me within seconds.

"Get on all fours" he instructed. However, when I couldn't move, he repositioned me himself. "Chelsea look at me" he whispered, "you've done the hard part. Just one last bit to go, and then comes all the good". His eyes looked into mine deeply, and for a moment I focused on the small golden specks in the darkness.

I nodded, drawing strength from Saxon's courage in me. He coached me through it, and I did everything that I was told. "Take a deep breath, and clear your mind" he began, taking a seat on the floor next to me.

"Now, imagine your foot. Picture it in your head, and imagine it growing and stretching. Good, good. Now the leg. It's growing and stretching. Yes, well done". He was calm, and quiet, but I was screaming as pain was exploding in every part of my body. "Right, and now your arms. Growing, and stretching, growing and stretching".

I screamed, and cried, and thrashed, as Saxon spoke about each part of my anatomy softly. I could feel my body changing, stretching and growing just like he said it would. It was painful, but I imagined it as more excruciating. And, then, just when I that thought entered my mind my back snapped.

I screamed the house down, and Saxon cringed as my back arched and my head was thrown back. In that moment I thought he was wrong – I hadn't survived the hardest part, as I was about to die. Because there was no way I could survive through that sort of pain.

But I did, my bones breaking and re-fusing themselves slowly. My toes and fingers were growing, and felt heavier at the same time my face began to tingle and I heard a 'pop' as my nose broke. I screamed again.

Then, just when I thought I was about to pass out, Saxon whispered right next to me. "It's over. You've Shifted". There was a heavy moment, where I didn't move. I stayed where I was, on all fours, with my eyes firmly shut. "Chelsea, open your eyes" he whispered, and I did.

Light streamed in, blinding me for a moment, before everything calmed down. Yet, everything looked different. Things were clearer, sharper, and more defined. It was like when you put someone's glasses on, and for a second everything is so clear, and then your eyes adjust and you have to pull the glasses away because their too strong. But there was no pull away – everything was sharp and crystal clear.

I glanced around the room, admiring everything with new appreciation. Then my eyes landed on Saxon. He sat next to me, suddenly a lot smaller than I remembered, with a manic grin on his face. "Chelsea" he whispered, but it was loud like he had shouted.

He looked so much more handsome with my new eyesight – glowing pale skin, darker freckles, eyes more vibrant than ever and teeth perfect and white. I tried to ask him about my eye sight, but all that came out was a whine and a growl.

Saxon laughed warmly, "yeah not being able to talk sucks. But you'll get used to it". He looked crazy, like he had just won the lottery. He looked so happy, that I couldn't help but feel happiness fester inside my. I had survived it all – I was a Werewolf.

I finally tore my eyes away from Saxon, and glanced down at my paws. I wobbled when I lifted one, and fell flat on my face. I growled out in annoyance, as Saxon laughed. I quickly repositioned myself, so I was sitting down on my hind, before I examined my paws.

They were large, and covered in thick black fur, with the bottom a thick rough surface. I had claws on each paw, which when I focused hard I could make extend and then retract. It was fun, I did that a few times.

Turning back to Saxon, I tried to ask him about a mirror. Again, just yips and growls came out. I frowned in annoyance, and Saxon chuckled again. "Mirror?" he questioned, guessing my thoughts. I nodded yes, and he got to his feet.

I must have been large, because when he stood up, he was only about a head taller than me. He opened his closet, to reveal a long mirror. He held the door open so I could admire myself. I gave a small growl of happiness at my reflection.

I was tall, and lean, with thick shiny black fur. My large, blue-green, eyes were large and bright. My muzzle was long, and thin, with a mouth full of sharp white canines. My legs were all thick, and muscled, and I had a bushy tail that hung between my back legs.

I jumped in shock, when Saxon touched my head. I skirted backward, with a yip of shock, before skidding and falling onto my muzzle. I hadn't quiet worked out the mechanics of moving on all fours. I whimpered in pain, as my jaw smacked off the floorboards.

"Shit, Chelsea" Saxon muttered, before kneeling down next to me. I sat back down on my rear, shaking my fur out. I gave a small snort of embarrassment, when Saxon chuckled at me. "Sorry, didn't mean to scare you" he laughed. Then he cautiously reached out and touched my fur.

I gave a soft purr as his hand ran down the span of my back – his hands threading through the strands of gentle fur. He offered me a bright smile, and just as he did, a knock sounded on the apartment door. Saxon froze, frowning deeply.

"Police open up" a male voice shouted. Saxon swore colourfully, whipping his head around to towards the bedroom door. "We have had complaints of a woman screaming from this address. Sir, can you please just open up the door".

"Wait here, and don't make a noise" Saxon whispered to me, before opening up the bedroom door and slipping out. He closed it behind him, before walking over to the apartment door and opening it up.

"Hello there, officer, is there a problem?" I heard Saxon asked. Panicking, I closed my eyes and tried to Shift back. But I didn't really know how to get back to my human form. Cussing mentally, I got onto all fours.

"We've had a few complaints of a woman screaming at this address" the police officer replied.

Saxon gave a warm laugh, "must have been a mistake. There's been no screaming here".

"Sir, do you mind if I come inside?" At that question, I knew that I had to focus to get back to my human form. The last thing Saxon needed was a cop finding a large Wolf in his bedroom.

So I cleared my mind, and pictured my human body. I imagined my body shrinking and changing, and soon I began to feel pain shooting through my limbs. I held all my pain in, not allowing myself to shout out.

"Do you have a warrant?" Saxon demanded.

"No. But let's put it like this, Sir, if you don't step aside I will arrest you for hindering my investigation and then I'll get the warrant. So if you have nothing to hide, Sir, please just step aside".

I felt my skin crawling, like with the bugs, and for a moment I panicked. When I did, the Shifting stopped. I mentally shook myself, before clearing my mind once more. I pictured my body, and it changing back. I let out a long breath, as the pain came shooting back.

"And do you live here alone, Mr Henderson?" the officer asked – walking through the lounge.

"Yes, Officer. Just me" Saxon replied. I felt my body tingling, and my head went light for a few moments.

"What's through here, Mr Henderson?" The voice was just outside the door. I was coming to the end of the change, my body almost human once more. I let out a groan of pain when it hit the last stage. "What was that?" the officer questioned.

"That's my bedroom, Officer" Saxon replied, and I heard a quick movement. I groaned, as I finished my Shift. My human body back and light. I let out a groan, as I stood up.

"Mr Henderson, move out of the way" the officer snapped, and I heard Saxon's breathing pick up. I stumbled to my feet, and grabbed a shirt from Saxon's closet. I pulled it on quickly, before rushing over to the bedroom door.

I ripped it open, to reveal Saxon's back with an officer in front of him. They both turned to look at me in shock – the officer because he hadn't expected me, and Saxon because he was shocked I was human again.

"Is there a problem, baby?" I asked Saxon, slipping my arm around his waist as I threw the officer a smile. "Hello, Officer, is there a problem here?" I battered my eyelashes.

"We've had complaints about a woman screaming" the officer frowned, glancing at my state of undress.

"Well that would have been me" I giggled, "sometimes I just can't control myself. Saxon just knows exactly how to make me scream". I giggled again leaning into Saxon, who blushed in embarrassment.

The officer cleared his through awkwardly. "As nice as that is, Miss. These were screams of pain".

"Oh I like pain" I smirked, eyes boring into the officer, who squirmed uncomfortably. "But if you want to check the bedroom, I can promise you that all they would have heard is me enjoying myself" I smiled.

I stepped out of the doorway, and Saxon slipped his arm around my waist as we allowed the officer to walk past us. "You're amazing" he whispered, too low for the police officer to hear. I offered him a grin, bright and giddy – and he mirrored the happiness. "My first Turn, and you're female. This is the best day ever" he grinned.

The officer had a look in the bedroom, and bathroom, before deciding that obviously I was the one screaming – and there was nothing suspicious to take further. He left minutes later. Saxon closed the door behind him, before turning to me with a bright grin.

He was in front of me in a second, wrapping his arms around me. I squealed in shock, and delight, and he twirled me around. I laughed as he put me down. "I can't believe this" he grinned. "My very own She Wolf Turn" he beamed.

Chapter Six

I slept in Saxon's bed with him that night, and then we woke up I dressed in a pair of his joggers – I had to tie them tightly, to fit around my thin waist. I then also wore a shirt that he had shrunk in the wash, it was still too big, but it stuck to my ample chest.

I looked myself over in Saxon's bathroom mirror. My long, dark hair fell into heavy waves to my chest. It looked shiner and softer than days ago. My eyes were also brighter and looked more alive. My body looked different too – my stomach tighter, my legs sturdier and my skin smoother. My large chest and wide hips were still the same.

Saxon had been beaming, and happy, all the night before and all morning. He couldn't believe that he had managed to find a woman who had survived the Turn. He never even considered the fact that he might be able to get a She Wolf for his Pack, yet he had, and he was ecstatic about it.

"You don't have to worry about money, or jobs, or anything anymore" he grinned, as I pulled my sneakers back on. "From today, Chelsea, you're part of the Pack. And we look after our own. So you never have to go back your job, or your shitty apartment, or to your cheating boyfriend. Today, Chelsea, is the beginning of your new life".

"You're cute when you're excited" I laughed, as I stood up and dusted my body off. Saxon beamed a bright smile.

"I am honestly so excited, you have no idea" he shook his head, still giddy with happiness. I just laughed as we headed out his apartment. Saxon and I were going to move all of my stuff out of my apartment, and into his storage. He told me that once we'd built the Pack up, he would help me get my own place – a nice place where I never had to worry about rent.

I gave Saxon my address, and he put it into the navigation system and started his car up. He spoke a few minutes into the drive. "What we'll do is I'll take you to the territory where my mother, and a few Pack members are. They'll train you to fight and--"

"What? No" I cut him off. "I want to come with you. I can help you find the others. And you can train me up on the road". I looked at him, eyes pleading. "You're my Sire, Saxon. I have to stay with you".

Saxon let out a long breath, fingers tapping the steering wheel as he thought. "Fine" he nodded, "but you have to do everything I say. You're young, and untrained, so you have to follow my lead no matter what. Understood?"

"I promise. Just please take me with you" I pleaded. Saxon smiled, glancing over at me, before nodding. Reaching over he gave my hand a squeeze, and it warmed me. I was never a tactile person, but with Saxon I didn't mind much. He liked to touch, and have physical contact, and I was fine with that.

It took us just under an hour to reach my apartment, which was on the other side of Toronto. It wasn't the nicest of places, but Saxon didn't comment or complain. He simply parked his car up, and helped me pack up my crappy apartment.

I quickly changed into a clean pair of jeans, and a shirt that cut half way up my stomach. I also changed my sneakers, for boots, as I thought the chance of forests was likely. I didn't own many things, so it didn't take Saxon and I long to pack it all into boxes and suitcases.

"All done?" I asked Saxon, as he rearranged all the furniture which came with the apartment. He nodded yes, moving the boxes over to the door with the others. A knock came on the door, and Saxon glanced at me. I shrugged my shoulders not knowing.

"Chelsea" a familiar shout sounded. I let out a groan. "I know you're in there you stupid bitch. Open this damn door now".

"That would be the cheating ex" I told Saxon, and he frowned. Before I could stop him, he walked straight to the door and opened it up. He crossed his muscled arms over his muscled chest, not looking happy.

My ex-boyfriend, Jamie, looked at Saxon in shock. Jamie was just as tall as Saxon, both of them reaching about six foot, but whereas Saxon bulged muscle from every part of him, Jamie had lean muscle. Jamie's dark black skin, made Saxon's paleness almost brighter in contrast. Jamie's right eyes was puffy, and bruising, from my left hook the night before.

"Who the fuck are you?" Jamie demanded, crossing his arms over his chest – his eyes glaring at Saxon.

"I was about to ask you the same question" Saxon replied, looking at Jamie like he was something on the bottom of his shoe. Jamie screwed his nose up at Saxon, before glancing around him to see me.

"Chelsea, who the fuck is this? And where the fuck is my car, you stupid bitch" Jamie growled, trying to step past Saxon. But, my Sire didn't even flinch as Jamie stepped up to him. "Dude, let me past". Jamie was getting madder and madder with each second.

"Chelsea doesn't want to see you" Saxon said calmly, a dangerous hint to his voice.

"How the hell do you know? Chelsea, come here and talk to me".

"Chelsea doesn't want to see you" Saxon repeated. "She doesn't have you car, and she doesn't want to be with you anymore". His voice was slow, and calm, like he was speaking to a small child. Jamie's forehead creased in anger, before his eyes glanced at the packed boxes at the door.

He actually looked worried. "Chelsea, what's going on? Where are you going? Who the hell is this?" He tried to look into my eyes over Saxon's shoulder – but Saxon wasn't moving any time soon.

"Saxon, give us a minute" I sighed. Saxon's shoulders tensed, and for a moment I thought he was going to fight me on the matter. But after a pause for thought, he turned to me.

"Shout me if you need anything. I'll start taking the boxes to the car" he told me, before scooping up an armful of boxes. He purposefully knocked into Jamie as he pushed past him. Jamie cussed at him, but Saxon just carried on walking.

Once Saxon was gone, Jamie turned to me – looking mad. "Chelsea, what the hell is going on here?"

"What's going on here, is that you cheated on me" I snapped, crossing my arms over my chest as I glared at him. Jamie's eyes looking down to my plunging cleavage for a moment, before he sighed heavily and looked away.

"I made a mistake, Chelsea. You know how I feel about you, I didn't mean to cheat. It just sort of happened. And it only happened once, I swear. Look, I know you probably won't forgive me but--"

"I won't" I interrupted. "Look, Jamie, it is over. It's not like we were serious anyway. We'd only be dating a few months. Saxon is an old family friend, and I'm moving away back with my family and--"

"You don't have any family" Jamie snapped, throwing his hands up into the air. "Fuck your none existence family. Where the hell is my car?" That was typical Jamie – he couldn't get what he wanted the nice way, so he went back to his aggressive ways.

"Your car is parked and a mile away from Helier Lake" I told him with a sigh. "Look Jamie, it's done. Will you just leave?"

"What no, I--" he began. But I was done with his shit. So I lunged forward, grabbing his shirt and with incredible speed and strength slammed him into the wall. Jamie yelped in pain, and I heard Saxon cuss before sprinting up the stairs.

"I said it's over Jamie. I told you where your car is. Now get the fuck out of my apartment". My face was pushed into his, and I my fingers dug into his shirt around his neck. I could see the shock, and fear, in Jamie's eyes.

Saxon rushed through the apartment door, and in one swift movement slipped his arm around my waist and pulled me away from Jamie. My ex muttered an oath, as he stumbled away from me. Saxon glared at him, as he held me to his chest. "Get out of here" he snapped at Jamie.

Jamie didn't say anything after that, he just glared at us for a moment, before sprinting out the door. I saw him run, and every part of my body wanted to go after him. My legs inched to chase him, to hunt him down, to--

"Breathe" Saxon whispered in my ear, cutting through my thoughts. "Deep breath, in through the nose, out through the mouth" he told me. I did exactly as he said, and focused on his hands resting around my waist. A few seconds later, I had calmed down. "Better?" he asked.

"Much, better, thanks" I sighed, as he let me go. "I just sort of lost it. Sorry".

"Don't be. You're a new Turn, your emotions are all over the place at the moment. It'll just take some time to get used to the animal instincts that are taking over your human instincts. Like the urge to chase your prey". He paused for a moment, "right. Ready to go?"

Chapter Seven

Once we had dropped all my stuff off in Saxon's apartment, and then I had packed a bag, we hit the road. I wanted to Shift again, but Saxon said to leave it a few days – let my body recover from the bite first.

The bite mark from Saxon, on my hip, had healed during my first Shift. Saxon explained that as Wolves we heal a lot better. So, if we're ever badly injured, we needed to Shift as soon as possible as our body will correct itself as best it can during the change of forms.

"So only a bite can Turn someone?" I asked, as Saxon and drove across the Canadian border and into the US.

"Yes, stories of scratches or sex with a Werewolf are all rubbish. Only a bite, as the saliva has to get into the bloodstream".

"So during rough sex…" I trailed off.

Saxon laughed loudly, "no. Has to be a bite in Wolf form. A Born has to be in Wolf form to successfully infect someone. So, rough sex no. Kinky sex possible, if they're into weird animal stuff".

I snorted in amusement. "So I'm guessing if there are hardly any female Wolves, then Borns have to marry humans".

"Correct. My mother is human, but she wasn't told about what my father was until after the marriage. That's the rules. Borns, and Turns as well, have to officially be married to a human before revealing their identity. It's the Council's rules".

"And the Council is made up of select Dominates in the world?" I questioned, and he nodded. I had so many things to learn, and so many questions still to be asked. I didn't want to keep bugging Saxon, but I was so interested I just wanted to know everything.

"So your father is a Dominate, and is on the Council?"

"Yes. My father is the Dominate of the US Pack. All the American Wolves are under my father's rules. Except Roamers of course. Roamers, are Wolves that are not part of the Pack. They are Lone Wolves, and don't belong to any Pack. However, if they break any of the Alpha's rules, my father is allowed to step in and punish them. Even though he's not their Dominate".

"So you're father's the Sheriff, but the Alpha's the Mayor" I mumbled.

"Exactly. The Alpha, and the Council, set the rules and it is the Dominates job to enforce it in their country" Saxon explained, and I nodded in understanding. "Right your choice. First stop New York, or straight through to Pennsylvania?"

"Straight through, but maybe we could get a drive thru at some point?" I smiled, and Saxon laughed. He had explained that Shifting took a lot of energy from the body, so the more times I Shifted, the hungrier I get. Which was why he suggested hunting during a Shift. And with my body still recovering from the Turn, Saxon had told me my body would be craving high protein and sugary foods for a while.

Saxon was hungry as well, so we grabbed some food quickly – and I was not too proud to order four large meals to myself. Saxon just laughed, and told me he liked a girl with an appetite. However, even he was shocked when I finished all the meals and then stole the last fries he didn't want.

By late evening, we had arrived in Pennsylvania. Saxon knew of a Wolf there, who wasn't in the Pack, but was a good friend of his. Apparently he was away, but Saxon had a spare key to his large mansion style home. And after the Police officer hearing my screams of pain, Saxon thought that a place away from others was best.

We would only stay there for two nights at most. Because either; we would kidnap someone and they would die, or we would kidnap someone and they would have to leave with us. Either way, people may question the missing person, and we didn't want to be caught up in a missing person case.

We pulled up at the house, glad to find it a small distance away from the other houses. We parked in the drive, and both climbed out the car. Inside the house, I was shocked by the horrible musky scent. "What is that smell?" I frowned.

"A Forced Turn" he told me, and I looked shocked.

"I told you that if you Force Turn, the person becomes violent and bloodthirsty. And they always do, but sometimes they can be saved by intense training. My cousin Chris, Forced Turned Dwight, about thirty years ago, but managed to train him to control himself. Father still keeps an eye on him, just in case he breaks".

"He smells musky, really earthy".

"More Wolf than human" he nodded. "Don't worry, soon you'll be able to work out different scents. You're senses are still developing. You're hearing is getting better, but you're still not up to the standard you should be as a Turn. But you'll get there".

Saxon and I put our bags in the spare room, planning to share the bed again. It was odd, but I had no problem with touching Saxon, or being naked with Saxon, or sleeping next to Saxon. He said it was because I was a Wolf – and we had a connection that went deeper than human instincts.

Pack Wolves didn't care about the human taboos. Saxon said half the time he shared beds with his brothers, both blood and Pack, and majority of the times they were naked or in compromising positions. Yet, to them it was completely normal. Wolves were close, and so were Werewolves. Wolves showed affection through touch and closeness.

Saxon decided the best time to hunt for a potential Turn, would be night. And I completely agreed. So we both dressed nicely; him in dark jeans and white shirt, and me in a tight black dress, before we headed out. We headed into central Pennsylvania, and quickly found a busy nightclub.

Saxon and I waited in line, before reaching the bouncer at the door. He checked our ID's before just checking me out, then let us into the club. "Does that not annoy you?" Saxon asked.

"What?"

"Having practically every guy you meet leer over you?"

"I was a stripper, Sax, I'm used to be sexualised. Plus, every girl gets it. It comes with having boobs" I smirked, as he pressed his hand to my back and urged me up to the bar.

"I bet it must be worse with curves like yours though. I mean, I know every girl has a chest, but not all of them are quite like yours" he said. I glanced at him, and he blushed scarlet.

"Yeah, I take after my mother. And you've seen me naked basically for the past forty eight hours, and you have not leered once". We reached the bar, and I smiled at the bartender to get his attention.

"Well not that you've seen" Saxon replied, mischievously smirking which made me laugh. Saxon ordered us both beer, which we then took to a small table on the second floor of the club. We managed to find a seat right on the balcony, which overlooked the dancefloor below.

"So what exactly are we looking for?" I asked, sipping my beer. My eyes looked over the busy club. I could see a range of different people; dancing woman in little clothing, men searching for a girl, men in suits just finished work, people who had been forced to come, people not drinking, people drinking too much. We had a lot of choice.

"Someone who won't be missed" Saxon replied, eyes looking over everything as well. I sipped my beer, wondering whether we'd soon be welcoming a new Turn or whether we'd soon be burying a body.

"Her?" I asked, gesturing to the slightly chubby girl hanging around the bar. She was obviously desperate for attention, but no one was even glancing at her.

"No. No more women. The Pack has you, we don't need another She Wolf".

"You can never recreate perfection" I commented, and Saxon smiled at my joke. I looked over the other dances, and the people sat at the bar. Looking back at Saxon, to see where he was looking, I saw someone behind Saxon.

He was leaning against a table of woman, trying to talk to them. Taking a deep breath, I tried to open up my hearing. Although, I knew already what the girls were saying. They were telling him they weren't interested.

The guy looked to be in his late thirties, possibly early forties, with a very average look. Some people would find him attractive, others may have thought he was too plain. He had swept back red hair, and a pointy chin. Not memorable, but not forgettable either. A happy medium.

When the woman rejected him, he headed over to a spare table and took a seat. He looked miserable, and I understood. He wished he was someone different, someone better. And Saxon and I could give that to him.

"Sax, him" I whispered, nodding behind him. Saxon inconspicuously spun in his chair, to see the man I meant. He turned back around smiling at me. "Perfect. Now how do we get him out of him?"

"With these" I pointed to my chest. Saxon chuckled softly. "I'll take him back to the house. Follow me home? At a distance of course".

He nodded softly, "sounds like a plan".

Chapter Eight

Taking my beer in one hand, I walked over to the man's table. My hips swished in an overtly sexual way, getting his attention before he even realised I was walking in his direction. When he realised I was heading straight for him, he sat up straighter, and I heard his heart speed up.

"Hey there" I smiled, reaching his table.

"Hi" he grinned.

"Can I?" I asked, pointing to the seat opposite him. His heart thumped happily again, and he nodded. I smelt something, and I quickly realised it was the smell of nervousness and sweat. His perspiration stuck to his forehead – and it was not just from the hot club.

I hopped onto the seat, making sure to swing forward enough that he got a nice eyeful of my cleavage. I knew how to use my body well. "What's your name?" I sipped my beer.

"Allan. What's yours?"

"Chelsea" I smiled, before we began to make the ideal chat. I told him I worked as a receptionist in a doctors – because I did that as a teenager, so I knew what to say without it sounding too much like bullshit.

Allan told me about his job, as part of a driving service, and I could tell he wasn't too interested in actually talking to me. His eyes seemed to spend the majority of the night on my chest, despite the compliments he paid to my eyes.

"Listen, I don't usually do this" I giggled, "but maybe you want to come back to mine for coffee?" I obviously said the right words, because his eyes lit up brightly.

"Yeah, sure. And just so you know, I don't usually do this either" he lied. We left our empty beer bottles on the table. I glanced back, looking for Saxon, but realised he was already gone. I wasn't shocked, because he needed to Shift to bite Allan.

Allan placed his hand on my lower back, before escorting me out the club. We walked the streets, the dark night surrounding us as Allan carried on the pointless conversation. There were butterflies in my stomach, and I couldn't tell whether it was because I was excited or nervous. Possibly both.

"This is a lovely house" Allan smiled, as I opened the door with the key Saxon had given me. As we stepped inside, I heard a low growl from the lounge. It was too quiet for Allan to hear, but I heard it – which I was supposed to. Saxon was letting me know he was ready.

"Allan" I said, turning on him. "Do you wish you were a different person? Someone stronger? Someone powerful?"

"I don't know" Allan stuttered, looking shocked. I stepped up to him, and he stepped back. "Why? Chelsea, you're scaring me". He stumbled back, when I stepped up to him again. His back touched the door, and his eyes widened in fear.

A floorboard creaked behind us, and Allan screamed in shock. I glanced quickly over my shoulder, to see a large midnight black Wolf. "We're going to make you like us, Allan. We're going to make you strong and powerful like us, Allan" I told him.

Allan screamed again, as the Wolf drew closer. Allan grabbed the handle, ripping the door open. I grabbed him, with strength I didn't realise I had, I pulled him straight back into the room and kicked the door shut. He screamed as I pushed him against the closed door, he groaned in pain as his back hit the wood.

Saxon gave a soft growl, before lunging forward and clamping his jaw over his Allan's wrist. He screamed bloody murder, and I rolled my eyes slightly. I had a feeling he was being a bit dramatic. Yes the bite hurt like a bitch, but I didn't act as pathetic as Allan.

Saxon moved away from Allan, who held his bleeding wrist. Saxon moved behind me slightly. Allan looked at me, eyes tearing up, before his knees buckled and he collapsed to the floor.

Saxon quickly shifted back, standing next to me naked. We both looked down at the unconscious man at the door. "Is that supposed to happen?" I asked.

"Don't think so" Saxon replied, "I think he fainted". His lips quivered into a small smile, and we exchanged a look. We both laughed for a moment, before sobering up. "I'll get changed, can you take him out to the garage?"

"Will do boss" I smirked, saluting him. Saxon headed back up the stairs, as I bent down and picked up Allan's limp body. I expected to struggle under his weight, but I was shocked with how light he felt with my new strength.

I took his body out to the garage, and dropped his body on the floor. He thumped down, body crashing into an awkward positioned. I straightened him up until a horizontal position, before pulling two plastic lawn chairs down from a pile of furniture in the corner of the garage.

I placed them down, as Saxon walked in with two beers in his hands. "A dead body and a beer. You know how to treat a woman" I teased, as we both sat down on the chairs.

Saxon chuckled darkly, "he's not dead yet".

"That didn't sound ominous enough" I laughed, and Saxon smirked softly. It was silent for a long while after that, both of us understanding the seriousness of the situation. I uncapped my beer and took a swig. I decided to change the conversation. "You know, I never drank this kind of beer before I came to the US".

"What do you mean?"

"My dad used to say if I was ever going to drink beer, it should be UK brewed or be cider. There was this quote from Monty Python that said; 'American Beer is a lot like making love on a canoe – it's fucking close to water'. Any every time anyone would offer him an American Beer he'd say that. And then my mother would hit him for swearing in front of me. So, out of principle, I didn't drink beer until recently". I gave a small laugh, taking a sip.

Saxon laughed, "they still live in England?"

"No they died nine years ago. Drunk driver" I replied soberly, taking another drink.

"Sorry".

"Yeah so I am" I smiled sadly. Saxon watched me for a moment – his eyes on my profile as I stay staring straight ahead.

"Do you mind talking about it?" he finally asked. I shook my head no, sighing heavily.

"I used to, when I was a kid. I mean when your fourteen and you're in a car crash. Then you wake up and find out both you parents died, it's like your life has ended. I moved in with my grandparents for roughly two years, but they said I was 'too wild' for them to cope with".

"Troubled kid?" Saxon guessed, and I gave a bitter laugh and nodded positively. "What did they expect? Your parents had both died, you were bound to be a handful".

I hummed, not convinced. "Anyway, when I was sixteen they decided I was too much for them. Shipped me off to live with my distance Uncle James. And he lived in Toronto with his Canadian wife".

"How was that?" Saxon asked, and I could hear in his voice that he genuinely cared. I paused, tongue running over my lips. "Chelsea" he whispered, placing his hand on my arm. "I'm your Sire, you can tell me anything".

"He didn't want to take his dead brother's troubled teenager. He had the perfect life. And I can't say anything bad about him. I mean, he looked after me and always tried to make me feel welcome. But it's hard when you're in a foreign country, with people you don't know, trying to make a sense of things you don't understand".

"What happened?" Saxon whispered, true concern his voice – a sound I hadn't heard for years.

"I forgot who I was. I dropped out of high school, drank too much, ran away, lived on the streets, got arrested a few times. Nothing major, but nothing good either. I just tried not to think about what my parents would think of their only child being a white trash stripper". There was venom in my voice, and Saxon noticed.

"You can make them proud now, Chels. You're only twenty three you have your entire life ahead of you. And you can make your parents proud, and you can make your Sire proud too". He gave me arm a squeeze, and I smiled at him.

A groan snapped us out of chat, and we both placed our beers down. Moving over to Allan, we both knelt down on either side of him. He was moving, as if waking, and a small smile edged onto Saxon's face.

Then, disasters struck. Allan's back convulsed – making us both stumbled backwards in shock. Allan began to make choking sounds, as he frothed at the mouth. Saxon cussed, and I mentally agreed. "Can we do anything for him?"

"Pray" Saxon replied grimly, moving away from where Allan carried on fitting. His body was writhing, his eyes were rolled back and the frothing was getting worse. I wanted to help, but I understood I couldn't.

Two minutes later his heart stopping beating. We'd killed him.

Chapter Nine

Saxon carried Allan's body over his left shoulder, as I carried two shovels. We put both of them in the back of Saxon's car and covered them over with a black tarp. "I can do this, you don't have to come too" Saxon muttered, as we closed the trunk.

"I'm coming, Saxon. No arguments about this" I replied sternly. My Sire nodded positively, before we both climbed into the car. We were both dressed warmly, as it was already one in the morning, and it was cold outside.

Saxon drove us to a secluded forest area, which looked dark and maze like. Thanks to my new heightened eyesight, I could see the path edged into the forest floor.

Saxon parked the car under a tree, and lifted the body out. I grabbed the shovels, and followed him into the forest.

We walked deep into the forestry – not staying to the path. Neither of us spoke, nor complained when it began to drizzle with rain. "This will do" Saxon finally said, after about thirty minutes of walking. He dropped the body to the ground, it made a horrible thump sound.

I handed Saxon a shovel, and we both began to dig. I couldn't believe how long it took to actually dig a hole deep enough; in the movies it always seemed pretty quick. But even with our strength, we were both tired and my entire body was aching, so it took us about three hours.

By the time Saxon announced it was deep enough, both of us were thickly covered in mud and debris. We both climbed out of the hole, before Saxon dropped Allan's body into it. We both paused for a moment, looking at the body at the bottom of his makeshift grave, before we began to cover him.

Another two hours later, we arrived back at the car. The sun was coming up, casting an eerie red light over everything. I frowned at the clock when it told me it was almost six in the morning. My body ached and I was tired – but my brain was too wired to even consider sleeping.

Back at the house, Saxon and I stripped all our clothing off. Saxon jumped in the shower first, as I threw our clothing into the washer, before scrubbing the mud off the bottom of our shoes.

Once that was done, I listened for a moment. I could hear Saxon moving around in the bedroom, and I knew just how stressed he was. Burying that body had not been easier for either of us, but Saxon had actually been the one to cause his death, and I knew it was eating him up inside. It was the first man he had killed.

Opening the cupboard, I planned to get us both some beers. I found something more interesting instead. I found Saxon pacing in the bedroom, still completely naked with water dripping from his form.

Saxon's nakedness didn't even make me blink. My thoughts about nude figures had changed dramatically. We both were naked, but there was nothing sexual about it. Werewolves thought of clothing as a hindrance, however, we had to wear them with humans. Saxon told me his Pack walked around naked most of the time – and it was the norm.

"Here" I smiled handing him the bottle. Saxon took the bottle and smirked.

"Tequila?"

"Thought we might need something to help us sleep. I'm going for a shower, start without me" I replied, and he chuckled softly as he uncapped the top. I had a hot shower, rinsing all the dirt from my body and under my fingernails. When I stepped out, I quickly dried myself and ran my hands through my wet curls.

Joining Saxon back in the guestroom, I took a seat on the bed next to him. He silently handed me the bottle, and I took a sip. I cringed at the pungent taste. "Arriba" I mumbled, and Saxon chuckled darkly. "Are you alright?" I questioned, taking another drink before handing the bottle back.

Saxon took a large gulp before answering, "I'm good". We both knew he wasn't.

"Yeah me too".

It was amazing we didn't wake up with a hangover the next morning – but Saxon said it was part of the Werewolf ability to burn through infection and antibodies quicker. Alcohol affected us as normal, the effects just didn't last as long as we managed to sober up quicker than a human. Which shocked me as we had drank a full bottle between us before passing out on the bed together.

The following morning, Saxon and I cleared the garage out and placed everything back where we'd found it. Saxon left Dwight a note saying he owed him one, and a replacement bottle of tequila. We then moved on.

We could still smell the hint of decaying body in the car, so we stopped to clean it out. No one else would be able to smell it, but our sensitive noses were plagued with the scent. Once we'd clean it out, had breakfast, and filled up with gas, we got back on the road.

"So do we try and find someone else in Pennsylvania, or wait until Virginia?" Saxon asked, driving slowly.

"Do you know anyone in Virginia to stay with?"

"No but we're heading up to Kentucky, where I do know some people. However, I want to have tried at least two more times for another Turn by the time we get there. So either we try twice in Virginia or we could try once more here first". Saxon was thoughtful, but there was a cold edge to his voice.

As much as he denied it, the death of his first attempted Turn was upsetting him. He blamed himself for Allan's death; and even though it was his fault, we were both to blame. "We'll wait until Virginia" I replied, reaching over and placing my hand over his on the wheel. "I choose him, Saxon, I am as much to blame as you".

"I bit him, just like I will bite all the others. I'm killing them not you".

"You're trying to save the Council, and all the other Werewolves in the world. Sometimes sacrifices have to be made". I leant over and pecked his cheek softly. Saxon offered me a small smile, before taking my hand which rested in my lap.

"My father will like you" he smiled, leaving our hands conjoined on my lap as we drove. "But, you are right, we have to do this to overturn the Alpha. It's just...I've never killed an innocent person before".

"And you still haven't killed anyone innocent, Saxon. Allan died because of an allergic reaction to your saliva. You didn't murder anyone". I gave his hand a squeeze, noticing how strong and callous his hands were.

"I wish I could believe that, Chels, I really do". Lifting our hands up, he pressed a gentle kiss to the back of mine, before letting them fall back into my lap with his conjoined. I couldn't help but get butterflies from his kiss, even though I knew it wasn't a sexual thing.

We stopped for lunch, to which I still ate loads, before we got back onto the road. Saxon had promised to take me for a run, and when we got to Hot Springs, Virginia, it was late night. I was getting sick of missing most of the day – but I was more excited to Shift and run with Saxon.

We brought a motel room, before Saxon drove us to a secluded woodland area. We parked our car up, and undressed in the dark. Adrenaline was running through my body, and I could hardly keep still.

Saxon smiled at me, amused by my childish attitude. Slipping his arm around my nude waist, he pulled me to his side. "Make sure you stay with me, and you listen when I try and tell you something".

"Promise" I grinned, hugging Saxon happily. He laughed, arms around me, as out naked bodies pressed together. "Come on, let's go". Taking his hand, I pulled him into the thicket of the dark forest. Giggling I ran ahead of him when he was walking too slowly.

"Chelsea slow down" Saxon sighed, but he was smiling. I turned around, so I was skipping backwards, and he shook his head at me. About five minutes later, Saxon came to a stop. "Here will be fine" he nodded, lowering to the floor.

I crouched down next to him, getting on all fours. "You go first" Saxon whispered, pushing my dark hair out of my face. "I'm right here". His hand ran over my back, and a shiver racked my spine.

Once more Saxon talked me through the Shift, and I listened and did everything he told me too. It just hurt like a bitch, but it wasn't anywhere nearly as painful as the first time. As soon as I my Shift was completed, I collapsed on the floor in exhaustion, my tongue lolling out the side.

Saxon smiled at me, before scratching behind my ear. I gave a growl of satisfaction, and he laughed at me. Once I got some more energy back, I stood up on my legs and stretched out – my hind in the air and my face dipping near the floor.

Saxon chuckled next to me, and I turned and gave his a wolfy smile. Reaching over I nudged him with my head, wanting him to Shift too. But, I still hadn't quiet worked out the mechanics of my new form. So, when I nudged into him it put me off balance and I topped onto him.

Saxon and I crashed to the floor; him making a noise of pain due to weight of me. I jumped off him, yipping in apologies, as I shakily got back on four legs. Saxon groaned as he lay on the floor. I whimpered softly before licking his face.

"Ow Chelsea, your tongue is like sandpaper. That hurts" he frowned. I whimpered again, trying to apologise without words. "You're sorry, I get it" he laughed, getting to his own position to Shift. "Chelsea move back and give me some room".

I made a noise of apology again, as I rushed backwards. I yelped once more and I moved to fast, and crashed to the floor. Saxon laughed, shaking his head at me. I quickly stood back up, and shook my fur out. "Don't worry, you'll get the hang of it" he promised.

I nodded, as he groaned in pain – his Shift beginning. I watched in fascination, as his body stretched and grew as he groaned in pain. However, whereas I had screamed and whimpered, Saxon just made small noises of pain.

When we were both Shifted, Saxon stood up with speed I envied. Turning to me, he growled softly before walking around me – looking over my body. My instincts didn't have a problem with him there, and I allowed him to sniff my rear and brush his wet nose over my body. When he was satisfied, he walked around back to my face.

Then, he took off running. I yelped in annoyance and I followed him clumsily.

Chapter Ten

Racing through the dark night, the forest around me, I couldn't help but fell happier than I had in years. The air brushed through my dark fur, making a whipping sound when I veered around corners. My eyes didn't have a problem with the dark – I saw even better than when it was day.

When I'd first started to run, I kept falling and crashing into things. I couldn't grasp the concept of running on four legs instead of two. Saxon huffed laughter the entire time, but always helped me up. It took me a while, but I realised the more I thought about it the harder I found it. So I cleared my mind, and soon I was racing Saxon around the forest.

We ran for a few hours, before Saxon began to get bored. Shocking me, he lunged at me as I ran forward, tackling me to the ground. I yelped in pain, as he pinned me to the floor. I growled at him, annoyed, before trying to get out of his grip. Finally, he let me go, before knocking me over again the moment I stood up.

I was angry for a while, when he kept doing, and after the fourth time I fought back against Saxon. He growled, happy, and it took me a moment to realise that was his goal. He wanted to fight with, to play with me.

So I played along, watching Saxon, and mirroring his actions. I watched the way he lunged, he jumped, he moved. I learnt his techniques and the way he fought with me – even if it was in a playful manner. Saxon was impressed, and we carried on playing fighting and wrestling. I knew he was going easy on me, but it still felt good when I was able to get the upper hand for a second or two.

As the sun came up, Saxon and I grew tired of the game. I was hungry, and with the way my Sire perked up at the smell of rabbits, I could tell he was too. The main thing that Saxon said I had to do since I was a Wolf, was give in to my instincts. He said my instincts would change to a more primal outlook of situations, and I had to let them.

So as soon as I smelt the scent of rabbits, and my stomach grumbled, I knew that I wanted to hunt that rabbit. Every part of me screamed at me to follow the scent, and to enjoy it. And when I saw Saxon take a large inhale of the scent, I knew he wanted the same thing.

I gave a soft growl, nodding my head in the direction of the scent. Saxon growled happily in return before running his head through my fur again – and I purred softly. We stayed like that for a moment, before Saxon slowly stalked through the forest and I followed behind him.

Saxon moved silently as death, stalking his prey like the skilled hunter he was. His paws treaded lightly, not even rustling the leaves covering the ground in a rusty autumn blanket. A soft growl rumpled my chest, my body wanting to pounce and hunt. I was impatient, and I didn't want to wait any longer for my kill.

Saxon glanced at me over his broad shoulder, his eyes telling me to be quiet or go hungry. I kept my teeth clamped together in a somewhat misguided attempt to keep my hunger muted. When he was happy I wouldn't scare his prey away, he turned back around.

His dark eyes peered through the night, zoning in on the two small rabbits to his left. Lowering his head a fraction, he eased his large form forward. Nodding discreetly with his muzzle, he directed me to come from the other side of the animals. My stomach flipped in excitement, as I shuffled around so I opposite him. Between us was a small collection of shrubs, with our prey in the middle.

I offered Saxon a toothy grin, excitement clear through my shiny pearly whites. Saxon just glanced at me, before looking away back at the prey. He was amused with my childish ways, but also annoyed as it was slowing the hunt down.

I inhaled the small of the rabbits, and my stomach growled in hunger. My mouth watered in anticipation for the fresh, bloody, meat I was about to devour. Saxon and I shared a look, before he pushed back so his weight was concentrated on his hind legs. I copied his actions.

And then, with a quick nod of his head, we both sprung forward. Like a giddy puppy, I flew higher than needed. Saxon was on his rabbits in record time, teeth instantly clamping around his prey's neck – an instant, clean, kill.

On the other hand, I landed beside my prey and alerted it of the danger. It shot off at a fast speed, but I was faster. With large paws I swatted the creature. It gave a small squeak, before collapsing to the floor. I dived on top of it, pinning it with my front paws. I gave a growl of happiness at having my catch.

The small rabbit froze in fear, heart racing at dangerous speeds. I revelled in the kill for a moment, adrenaline boiling through my bloodstream. Saxon gave a growl of annoyance, telling me to stop playing with my food and just kill it. I growled back in anger, but quickly used my jaw to snap the rabbit's neck.

Saxon moved closer to me, placing his meal in front of me. He took a step back, leaving his kill with mine. I gave him an odd look, as he sat away from me, and placed his head near the floor. I smiled happy, realising he was giving me his meal. He must have been proud of me.

I ate the meat, blood spraying all over my fur and face. It was messy, but I didn't care. I left a bit of the meat left, before dragging it over to Saxon. I offered it to him, and he gladly tucked it. I watched as he ate the meal, no mess anywhere on him. Which was almost humourless, especially when he glanced at the blood matted into my fur with a roll of his eyes.

Padding over to me, Saxon began to clean my fur for me – his pinkish, rough, tongue running through my dark fur. I shivered, as I allowed him to groom me. I liked him grooming me, it was almost pleasurable. I made a soft purring sound to show how much I liked it. Saxon chuckled, as he rubbed his head against my neck.

When he was finished grooming me, he nodded for us to head back. I grumbled in annoyance, but begrudgingly agreed. We trotted slowly back towards the car; dawn breaking around us.

Shifting back was painful, and the more I thought about the pain, the worse it got. I reminded myself that I needed to clear my mind; I had to let my body take control as it knew how to get me through the Shift.

"It gets easier, Chels, I promise" Saxon told me, once the Shift was over. I was on all fours, breathing heavily, as sweat poured from my face. I never used to sweat much before the change, but since then I was applying deodorant a few times a day. Saxon kept telling me to stop, that I wasn't sweating any more than before, I could just smell it better.

No matter the reason, I felt disgusting. I smelt fresh – and not in the good way. Yet, Saxon didn't even seem to notice. He simply offered me a hand, before pulling me to my feet. I wobbled, out of fatigue, so he slipped his arm around my waist to help me take my own weight.

"That was fun" I breathed out, as we headed back towards the car.

"It was. You're a fast learner" he praised.

"A messy eater though".

He laughed, "but you're still young".

We quickly reached the car, and redressed, before driving back to the motel. I chatted the entire way back, not being able to keep quiet. I had loved being in Wolf form, I had never felt so free and happy.

"I'm glad you enjoyed it" Saxon nodded, as he stopped the car. He gave me a small smile, but it was an almost sad smile. I gave him a look of confusion.

"Have I done something?" I asked, worried as I turned to look at him. The light from the motel sign sending a yellowy glare over Saxon's sharp profile. He sighed, before turning to me with another sad smile.

"You have done nothing wrong, Chelsea. You are the perfect She Wolf. My father will be extremely happy with having you as part of the Pack, and no doubt every male Wolf you come into contact with will instantly fall in love with you. I'm just…I just wish the circumstances were different".

"What do you mean?"

"I want to just stay here, and teach you to fight and to hunt. But we can't because I have to make more Turns. And I just…I don't even know, I'm just struggling with all of this. I don't want to do this anymore". He gave a small shrug, and I could see the pain in his eyes.

"*You* don't have to do this, Saxon. *We* have to do this". I reached over and took his hands in mine. "We're a team now, Saxon, and everything we are do together". I looked at him, his dark eyes hooded and tired. He gave my hands a squeeze, but he still didn't look convinced.

Chapter Eleven

The term 'lucky number three' didn't count for burying bodies. By the time we got to Kentucky, we had still not managed to turn anyone. We'd stayed in Virginia for three days – a different motel each night – but we had lucked out on all of them.

Our second attempt had been a maths teacher, recently divorced, named James. His body had been buried in the woods, and the following day we buried an ex-drug dealer named Keith. Neither of them had made it through the initial bite. I picked both men up in bars.

With each death, Saxon seemed to age further and further. All the death was weighing on his consciousness, and with each passing death, the Saxon I knew was disappearing slowly. His smile was almost non-existent by the time we got to Kentucky.

One of the Pack members lived just outside of Georgetown, and Saxon was going to take me there for a week. He had planned to use the week to train up all his Turns, but unfortunately, I was the only Turn he could train up.

Saxon was silent, as we drove through the narrow streets, towards the Pack member's house. His hands were tightly wrapped around the steering wheel, with his arms straight and tense. His jaw was sharper, where he was biting down on his molars.

"Saxon" I whispered, my voice cracking with emotion. My Sire looked over at me, the beautiful brown eyes softening as he took me in. "We'll find some I promise. I know it's hard, but we'll manage at some point I promise".

Saxon offered me a strained smile, "I know we will, Chels. I'm just not used to all this killing. Which sounds ridiculous since I'm a PI and I spend my life clearing up Werewolf murders and hiding the evidence of failed Turns. Yet they never seem to bother me. But, with these people that *I* am killing, just the look of their bodies makes me queasy".

"Of course it will, Saxon. You're not a psychopath, you have feelings". I leant over and pressed a lingering kiss to his cheek. "We'll get there, Sax, I promise". Pulling back, I willed him with my eyes to believe me. He gave me another smile, the second one more genuine.

"Ernie's house is only about five minutes from here" Saxon said after a while.

"And Ernie is another Pack member, right?"

"Ernest is my oldest brother. He's next to take over as Dominate of the US Pack, when my father's ready to retire.

Or, hopefully, when he becomes Alpha" he explained, and I nodded in understanding. "Ernie's wife is a lawyer, she's away at the moment, so it'll just be the three of us".

"Does he know we're coming?"

"He's knows I'm coming with a new Turn, but doesn't know you're a female". He chuckled softly, the lazily half smile he had been missing since the deaths began, fell onto his lips. "I can't wait to see his face".

I laughed softly, "I'm sure it'll be a shock".

The car followed the twisty, narrow, lanes towards a large house on the top of a hill – a small forest backing onto the house. It was late evening, the sun setting in the distance, and the day darkening into night.

Ernie's house was a large, modern style, eco build. The majority of the house made out of wood, and recycled materials, with the entire back of the house made up of large glass windows.

As Saxon rolled the car to a stop, killing the engine, the light on the porch flicked on brightly. Saxon got out first, and I followed suit, before we both grabbed our bags from the trunk. The door was left unlocked, so we walked inside casually.

"Ernie?" Saxon shouted for his eldest brother. There was a pause, before the sound of footsteps echoed overhead. I closed the door behind me, as the smell of fresh pine from the house's frame filled my sense.

"Pup? That you?" a deep male voice called back, a chuckle making the words teasing. I glanced at Saxon, who almost flushed in embarrassment of the nickname.

"Yeah it's me" he grumbled back. He obviously didn't like to be reminded that he was the youngest of seven brothers. I didn't mind, I thought it was sweet that his brothers teased each other. I was an only child, so had never had that bond, so I thought it was endearing.

Saxon's brother bounded down the stairs, with a large grin on his face. He looked to be in his early forties, with the same brown hair and eyes as Saxon. However, his hair was greying on the edges and his jaw wasn't as sharp. Whereas Saxon was broad and muscled, Ernest was tall and lean.

"Hey Pup" he beamed at his brother, before he skidded to a stop when he noticed me. He pause in the middle of the staircase, his eyes on me. Taking a deep inhale, he took notice of my scent. Then, he grinned like a maniac.

Turning back to Saxon, he shook his head in shock. "You are going to become Dad's new favourite" he laughed, jogging down the rest of the stairs to greet us. Saxon laughed at his brother, before they shared a manly hug. Then, Ernie turned to me. "And who is this beautiful new Turn?"

"Chelsea" I smiled, offering him my hand. He glanced down at my extended hand, laughed, and pulled me into a hug. I instantly hugged him back, noticing how his scent smelt very similar to Saxon's – just not as earthly. Usually I didn't hug people when first meeting them, but Ernie was a Pack brother, and I instantly relaxed into his hold.

"Well aren't you a looker" Ernie smiled, pulling away and holding me at arm's length. "Saxon you better lock the other Wolves up before you start taking her around the country. Every Wolf in a hundred miles will be wanting to be her mate". His eyes twinkled in mischief.

"I'm sure Saxon and I could take them on" I smirked, and he laughed.

"And with an accent like that". He gave a low whistle of appreciation. "You better keep your eye on her, pup". He let me go, and Saxon slipped his arm around my waist instantly. Ernie noticed the movement, and his already bright smile seemed to double.

Even though they looked similar, they were polar opposite when it came to their personalities. Even though Saxon was warm, and caring, he was a serious man. Yet, Ernie didn't even look like he had ever frowned.

"You kids hungry?" Ernie asked, waving us through his house and to the kitchen.

"I could eat" I nodded, as Ernie raided the freezer. Our options were frozen pizza or frozen lasagne. However, after a small discussion, we cooked both. Ernie stuck them in the oven, set the egg timer, and then bustled us into the lounge.

"So are the other Turns close behind?" he questioned, as he sat in a large armchair and we perched on a couch. Saxon's smile dimmed, and I quickly swept in.

"Just me at the moment. We'll get some more soon" I shrugged the conversation off, slipping my hand into Saxon's. His fingers wrapped around mine, giving them a squeeze, as his brother got up.

"Fair enough. Drinks?" He opened a glass cabinet and pulled three small crystal glasses out.

"You got any bourbon?" I questioned.

"Of course" he nodded, pulling a bottle out of the back of the drink cabinet. He poured us both a glass, before pouring on for himself. "You kids are old enough to drink, right?" he teased.

"Shut up" Saxon grumbled, as I just rolled my eyes at Ernie. He beamed another cheeky grin, laughing at his own joke, before taking a seat once more. I took a sip of the whiskey, letting it warm me slightly as it flowed through my body. We talked aimlessly for about thirty minutes – just Ernie getting to know me.

"So Chelsea what do you do for a job?" Ernie asked.

"Nothing at the moment" I replied, smiling at him. "Once we get our Dominate as Alpha, I'll have a look at what I want to do with my life. But until then we have too much to do".

"Our father is going to love her, pup" Ernie laughed.

"I know" Saxon laughed too.

"So" I changed the subject, "when do we start training?" I was eager to learn to fight and understand my new body. I couldn't wait for Ernie and Saxon to start training me – I was like a kid in a candy shop.

"We'll start in the morning" Saxon replied, sipping on his own glass.

Once we'd eaten, and Ernie had shown us to our rooms, I retired to bed. As I showered, I could hear the brothers talking downstairs. It was hard to hear them with the running water, so I slipped out the shower – leaving it running so they didn't hear me – and moved closer to the door. I strained my hearing.

"She's pretty" Ernie commented. Saxon didn't reply for a moment. "You like her" his big brother taunted, and butterflies dipped in my stomach.

"Of course I do, she's my Turn and I'm her Sire" Saxon replied nonchalant.

"You know that's not want I mean, Pup. Plus, there aren't many Wolves who can say they have been with a She Wolf. There is only four in the world, well, five now including Chelsea. You'd be stupid not to go for it, Pup. Not to mention she is beautiful. Those eyes, and of course those boobs".

"If you like her so much why don't you date her?" Saxon snapped angrily – in a tone I had never heard him use before.

"Easy, Pup, no need to get possessive. You're her Sire, so she will always have feeling for you and--"

"What do you mean she'll always have feelings for me because I'm her Sire?"

"Think about it. Dad's our Sire, and when he asks something we all fall over ourselves making sure it's done. She will be the same to you. You ask for something, she'll do it. That Sire bond is unbreakable, Saxon. So if you wanted to date her, she would do it in a heartbeat".

Saxon was quiet for a long while, and I wanted badly to see his expression. "I'm going to head to bed" he finally said, after a good few minutes of silence. I then heard him walking up the stairs, so I slipped back into the shower silently

Chapter Twelve

I couldn't sleep in the bed on my own, and for a few hours I tossed and turned. When the early morning came, I realised that sleep was not coming. So I clambered out the bed, wearing my pyjamas, and silently crept out to the corridor.

I walked down to Saxon's room, and lightly knocked on the door. I heard an incoherent grumble, and I cautiously opened the door. Saxon lay in the bed, hair tousled and eyes heavy. "Can't sleep?" he asked around a yawn.

"The beds really big" I mumbled, a red tinge of embarrassment burning onto my cheeks. Saxon nodded in understand, and simply held the covers open for me. I closed the door behind me, before walking over to the bed and slipping inside.

I curled into Saxon's arms – the familiar warmth of his body instantly putting me at ease. I hadn't slept without him in almost two weeks. I had grown accustomed to him being there. I rested my head on his bare chest, as his arms slipped around my waist and held me close.

"I didn't mean to wake you" I muttered, my body fighting the sleep off already.

"I wasn't sleeping either. Just resting really, too restless to sleep. Kept waking up".

"Why?" I asked, through a yawn of my own.

"Just thinking" he replied with a shrug. I should have pressed the subject really, but I was so tired that I just muttered something that didn't really make any articulate sense, before falling asleep.

The following morning, the smell of strong coffee woke both Saxon and I up. We both stumbled out of the bed, and were guided by our noses down to the kitchen. Ernie sat at the island, reading the paper with a cup of coffee in his hand.

"Morning kids" he grinned a toothy smile.

"Coffee" I mumbled, letting him know I wasn't going to function until the caffeine buzz had kicked in. I poured both Saxon and I mugs of coffee, before we sat down on the island opposite Ernie.

As I drank my coffee, and Ernie read his paper, Saxon stuck some bacon in the pan before scrambling some eggs. He quickly served the three of us some food, and we ate in silence. "Not a morning person, huh?" Ernie smirked at me.

"I didn't get much sleep last night" I shrugged, chomping on slightly salty bacon. "Plus the caffeine hasn't got into the bloodstream yet" I added, and Ernie chuckled softly. I finished the last of my breakfast, before standing up. "I'll go get changed, and then we'll start training?" I asked eagerly.

"Sounds good" Ernie beamed, finishing his own meal. I smiled happily before bouncing up the stairs. I quickly changed into my work out kit, before jogging back downstairs. The brothers were still chatting in the kitchen.

"Saxon" I whined, "go change". I pouted my lips childishly, as I battered my eyelashes at him. Saxon laughed at me, before placing his coffee down and heading out the door. He pressed a playful kiss to my cheek as he left, before he jogged upstairs. "You too Ernie" I pointed the other Pack member to the stairs.

He laughed, "alright, alright, I'm going". His hands held up in mock surrender, as he gulped the last of drink down, before heading to his bedroom.

When both men came back down, they were dressed ready for a workout. I couldn't help but jump up and down on the spot. Saxon laughed, as his slipped his arm around my waist, and led me out to the garden.

The large yard backed onto the forest; the scents sending my nostrils flaring as I stepped outside. Saxon led me into the centre of yard, before moving his arm away from me. "Ready?" he grinned, his face looking almost identical to his happy-go-lucky eldest brother. I nodded yes, and Saxon pressed another kiss to my cheek.

They spend the day teaching me to fight – beginning with defensive moves before moving onto offensive moves. My punches were something I was good at, from years of defending myself against abusive boyfriends and people with grabby hands at the strip club. But my kicks were something I couldn't control.

But after a few days of continuous training, I was holding my own against both elder Wolves. Both of them were impressed, and Saxon kept laughing that soon I would give all his brothers a good fight. On Thursday morning, Saxon went out to Shift as Ernie and I sparred.

Lunging forward, Ernie raised a fist at me. I ducked, pivoting on my back foot so I could dance backwards. I straightened up, aiming my own punch at him. He dodged, so I followed up with a roundhouse kick to his abdomen. He groaned in pain, stumbling back a step.

In his moment of weakness I tried for another punch, aiming for his chest. But, Ernie was fast, and he darted to the left. The quick movement made me pause for just a second, and Ernie took the opportunity to deliver a swift kick to stomach.

I hit the floor, my leg snaking out as I went – sweeping his legs away like bowling pins in an alley. He cussed as he went down, arms not being quick enough to brace himself. He landed on his rear, just as I straightened myself up.

I dived at Ernie, flattening his body to the ground before he's fully recovered from the fall. My hands grabbed his wrists, and quickly restrained him, before flipping him around so he was face down. I roughly pulled his arms behind him back, as I straddled him. "And you, sir, are under arrest" I joked.

He laughed from under me, which made both of us shake. "Nice work, kid. Although I am pushing forty-two so I'm not really well matched to a teenager".

"I'm twenty three" I pouted, giving his hands a tug in annoyance. He groaned in pain, but also gave a warm laugh. I held him for a little while longer, before releasing him and standing up. "Need a hand up, old man?" I chuckled.

"Funny" he laughed, taking my hand and allowing me to pull him to his feet. We both dusted ourselves off, slight mud from the yard caked into our clothing. Just as I was walking back towards the house, Ernie sprang at me.

I yelped in shock, as his leg thrust out and kicked into my stomach. I doubled over in pain, and as I groaned, he grabbed my legs and pulled them from under me. I fell on my rear, with another shout of pain. Ernie grinned down at me. "Age before beauty, kid". With that he threw me a wink, and a signature grin, before he swaggered into the house.

I growled lowly to myself, grumbling in annoyance, as I pulled myself back to my feet. I cussed Ernie out under my breath, but I was more annoyed at being caught off guard than anything. "Come get your breakfast, kid" Ernie shouted, laughing from the kitchen.

Saxon and Ernie had told me I needed to eat a healthier diet with all the training I was doing. So they were both making me drink disgusting health smoothies, and high protein meals – but I didn't mind because it meant they both did all the cooking. And they were both amazing chefs.

I took a seat on the kitchen table, and Ernie placed a funky looking green drink in front of me. I must have look afraid, as Ernie boomed a laugh out. "It's just kale, spinach and mint. Don't look like I just served you a raw deer".

"I'd rather have the raw deer" I replied, reminding of the meal the three of us had hunted the night before. Ernie chuckled, as he began to fry up something that I really didn't like the look of. "What the hell is that?"

"It's black pudding. I thought you brits love this thing".

"Well I certainly don't. It looks disgusting" I replied, and Ernie laughed before mimicking my accent. I glared at him, as I choked the health shake down. As Ernie placed the black pudding in front of me, I felt my stomach turn, but after a few bites I couldn't deny that it looked worse than it tasted.

As we finished eating, the front door flew open manically. "Chelsea, Ernie" Saxon shouted manically. The two of us were out of our seats in seconds, and racing towards our Pack brother.

Out at the front door, a naked Saxon gave us scared looks before he dropped a body in front of us. We both cussed, as we looked at the man Saxon had just bitten. He looked to be in his early thirties, with swept back red hair. What made us both worried, was the fact he wore the full cop uniform. Saxon had bitten a cop.

Chapter Thirteen

"Let's get him into the garage" I spoke up, breaking both men from their horror. They both looked at me in shock, my words not registering. So I repeated them once more; before following my own instructions.

Saxon picked up the cop's body, and hoisted him over his broad shoulder. I closed the front door quickly, flicking the lock, before running out to the garage. Saxon was placing the cop down, as Ernie was reversing his car outside to give us some room.

"I didn't mean to. I swear I didn't have a choice" Saxon rushed, voice full of urgency for me to believe him. I put my arms around him, burying my face in his neck. His arms wrapped around me, hands holding me tightly. "I'm sorry. I'm so sorry" he breathed out shakily.

"I know you are" I whispered, pressing a kiss to his neck. "I know you, Sax, and I know you wouldn't have done this unless you had a real reason too". I trailed my kisses up his neck and to his ear. My lips seemed to calm him, and he shivered against me.

"You better have a good explanation, pup" Ernie growled angrily, as he walked back into the garage, and shut it behind him. I pulled my head out of Saxon's neck, but kept my arms around him. Ernie looked pissed; a look that really didn't suit him.

"I was hunting in my Wolf form. I was thinking, and I wasn't really paying attention to anything. And I didn't realise I had gone so south, until I heard the barrel of a gun click. And then I turned around, and he was pointing a shotgun at me. I freaked out, and lunged at him. I was going to kill him…but I couldn't" Saxon explained, voice breaking at the end.

"So you bit him instead?" Ernie demanded.

"No. I knocked him to the ground, and ran for it. But he recovered quickly, and shot me. It caught the back of my thigh". His words terrified me to my core, and I pulled away to check out his thighs. But there was nothing wrong with them, not even a limp when he walked. "I was bleeding badly. So I had to Shift back, so that the muscle and skin would repair itself".

"He's fine Chelsea" Ernie assured me, as I ran my hands over Saxon's thigh. I nodded, standing back up and letting Saxon wrap his arms around me again. No doubt both men could hear my racing heartbeat, as I thought of Saxon being hurt and me not being there.

"I was Shifting back, and he found me again. I knew what I had to do, because I was half way through the Shift, and he saw. So I jumped on him, bit him, and knocked him out. I wasn't sure what else to do".

"You had no choice, Sax. He tried to kill you even when you weren't a threat" I told him, pressing a lingering kiss to his chest – next to where I was resting my head.

"I told you to be careful, Saxon" Ernie snapped. "The town over have a Wolf cull on. If they see a Wolf, they are obliged to kill it, because they have been killing the farmer's life stock. The cop was just doing his job. I told you not to go too far south".

"I'm sorry, Ernie" Saxon whispered, hand hanging in a childlike disappointment. I gave his waist a squeeze, telling him I was on his side, and I believed he did the right thing.

"What are we going to do? As soon as they realise a cop is missing, they'll search the woods for him. And where does those woods lead to? My fucking house, pup. I have spent the last twenty years making sure I kept a low profile so I could Shift in these woods and now you've fucked that up royally".

"That's enough Ernest" I snapped, not liking the way he spoke to my Sire. Both men looked at me in shock – not expecting my angry tone. "It's done, there is nothing we can do about it now. Saxon, you go and shower and change. Ernie, you have a basement right?"

"Sure. Full of crap though".

"Clear it out, and we'll put him down there. And we'll just have to prey he makes it through the bite and the fever" I told them. Both men nodded at me in a sync, before disappearing out the garage – leaving me with the unconscious cop.

I took a deep breath, before walking over the cop. His red hair was long, swept back with gel and blood, and his face was long and square. He was attractive, but in an unusual way. I bent down beside him, and quickly looked through his pockets for his ID.

I found his wallet in his pocket, and pulled it out. "Gavin Lorraine" I read off his ID, before slipping his entire wallet into my back pocket. I then put my fingers to his neck, and felt for his pulse; it was still going strong.

Once Ernie had cleared the basement out, we carried his body down there, and placed him on a mattress. "Don't be so hard on Saxon" I whispered to Ernie, as we put Gavin's body down. "He didn't mean to, he was scared".

"Saxon is not a kid, Chelsea" Ernie snapped at me. "He knows better than to go around biting cops. Just because you're in love with him, it doesn't mean you should baby him. He fucked up, and you pretending otherwise is not helping".

I blushed at his words, which weren't exactly untrue. I wasn't in love with Saxon, but it was definitely heading in that direction. "Don't speak to her like that" Saxon snapped from behind us. I turned to see him standing in the doorway, and I blushed deeper as I realised he had also heard Ernie's words.

"It's fine, Sax" I reassured him.

"No it's not. He can speak to me like that, because he's my oldest brother, but he doesn't get to speak to you like that. He can be a bastard to me, but he doesn't have the right to speak to you like that". Saxon walked to my side, and slipped his arms around my waist. I cuddled into his side instantly.

"I'm sorry Chelsea" Ernie sighed, pinching the bridge of his nose. "Saxon is right, I don't have the right to speak to you like that. I'm just…I'm just angry". He let out a soft growl of annoyance, and Saxon seemed to gain another frown line.

Gavin gave a groan, and we all jumped in unison. Spinning on my toes, I turned to face him. He was beginning to wake up, and with the sweat gathering on his brow, I had a feeling his fever was already beginning.

"Gavin?" I questioned, perching on the discarded mattress next to him. Large hazel eyes looked up at me, in both confusion and fear. "Gavin, my name is Chelsea, and I'm not going to hurt you".

"What--" he grumbled, voice hoarse and thick.

"Can you grab him some water?" I asked Saxon. Gavin followed my line of sight, and made a noise of fear when he saw Saxon and Ernie – no doubt the large, muscled, men did nothing to calm his nerves. My Sire quickly ran out to grab a glass of water from the kitchen. "Gavin I promise you, you're safe. We're down here because we don't want you to hurt yourself".

"Why would I hurt myself?" he asked, voice still strained.

"You were bitten, Gavin, by a Wolf. But it was not just any Wolf, it was a Werewolf. You're going to become like us, Gavin. And it's not a nice process, so we have to make sure we keep you safe while you go through it".

Saxon appeared with a glass of water, so I offered it to Gavin. He took it with shaky hands, taking a long sip. I took the glass out of his shaky hands once he lowered it, and placed it on the ground next to the mattress.

"Werewolves? They aren't real" Gavin argued, shaking his head manically.

"I used to think that too, Gavin, but now I am one. We are real, and you're going to become just like us. You just have to get through the fever first" I told him, trying to use a motherly tone, which was hard as I wasn't really maternal.

"Fever?" he choked out.

"The fever is a delirious stage, where your body is changing. It's hard, but you need to fight through it. Can you promise me you'll fight, Gavin?" I offered him a small smile, as he stared into my eyes. I was speaking fast, as the fever could start any minute.

"I'll try" he whispered, large hazel eyes glistening. "And I'll turn into a Wolf?" He still didn't look convinced so I knew one of us would have to Shift. I turned to Saxon, and he nodded in understanding.

"Saxon is going to Shift to show you, alright Gavin?" I said, as the cop coughed deeply. I handed him the last of the water as Saxon removed his clothes, and got onto all fours. Gavin was scared, but he was trying not to be.

I took the empty glass from him, and then took his hands in mine. Gavin gripped my hands tightly, and I could feel the sweat laying his clammy skin. Saxon groaned in pain, as he Shifted behind us – the sound of his breaking bones and stretching muscles filling the room. The cop whimpered, as Saxon's fur began to sprout over his skin.

As Saxon finished his transformation, and Gavin sucked in a heavy breath at seeing the large Wolf that used to be a man. "He won't hurt you Gavin, I promise" I told him, as his hands shook around mine.

"That will happen to me?" he whispered, staring at Saxon with eyes that glistened with unshed tears.

"Yes. But only if you fight the fever. Will you promise to fight the fever?" I asked. He nodded positively, and I offered him a bright smile.

"Will you stay with me, Chelsea?" he asked.

"Of course I will, Gavin. I'm not going anywhere until you're healthy again" I promised, and his eyes looked at me brightly – he believed me, and I promised myself I wouldn't let him down.

Chapter Fourteen

The fever hit Gavin about thirty minutes later. I had been through it, and I knew how horrible it was, but watching it was a different experience all together. Every time Gavin moved, my heart skipped a beat, and every time his breath caught so did mine.

It started out with him sweating badly, so I removed his clothing and placed ice packs all over his body. He was whimpering, as his skin was scoring a red colour as the sweat clung to the mattress below him. With a damp cloth, and a bucket of ice, I kept wiping his sweat away – just so it could be replaced with more seconds later.

"Chelsea I'm scared" Gavin whimpered, voice small like a child. His ID had told me he twenty eight, but in that moment he looked like a young boy.

"I know. I'm scared too, Gavin. But I'm here, I promise, I'm not going anywhere" I told him, wiping his wet hair out of his face. He gave me a small nod, as his hands grasped mine desperately.

"You better hope he survives, pup" Ernie growled at his brother behind us.

"And what if he doesn't?" Saxon asked, voice small and unsure.

"Then you'll be buried along with him" his elder brother snapped bitterly. Gavin's hazel eyes looked at me in fear; the mention of him being buried was not something that comforted him at all.

"Both of you get out" I snapped, glaring at them both of my shoulders. Ernie didn't argue, just turned on his heels and stormed back up the stairs. Saxon lingered, unsure, with a face full of anxiety. "I'll be right back" I told Gavin, before letting go of his hand. He whimpered in fear as soon as I was no longer holding him.

I walked over to Saxon, and led him up the stairs. I shut the basement door behind us, as I leant against it. "I'm the only one he trusts, Sax. I have to stay with him. You got me through the fever, and now I need to get him through it".

"I know" Saxon sighed, he seemed to have aged ten years since that morning. "But I don't want him to hurt you". Reaching up, I cupped his cheek gently – he leant into my palm.

"I'll be fine, Sax, I promise. If he gets out of hand, I'll call you down straight away". I pressed a long kiss on his cheek, as he hugged me close to his chest. "You did the right thing. I would have done the same in your situation. I know Ernie doesn't like it, but it's done now. Gavin was bitten, and we have to deal with it. Stop beating yourself up". I pressed another kiss to his check, wishing it was his lips, before pulling away.

Back in the basement, Gavin gripped my hand the very moment I sat down next to him. He was crying silent tears, as his entire body shook and sweated. We were quiet for a long while, before his eyes rolled back into his head.

"Gavin" I whispered, shaking him softly. But he was obviously in some sort of vision, because he wasn't answering me at all – yet his heart beat was even, and his breathing was only slightly laboured.

Ten minutes later, he began to scream and thrash. I moved so I was straddling him; pinning his limbs to the ground with mine, and using my supernatural strength to stop his movement. "Gavin come back to me. Gavin, I need you to come back to me".

He screamed, entire body moving and fighting with me – yet it was still easy to hold him. Gavin's eyes were open, the hazel iris bright and wild, as they glazed over. He stared at nothing and everything all at the same time. It was unnerving.

It must have been about half an hour, before Gavin stopped fighting with my hold and his eyes blinked before focusing on me. "Where am I?" he asked, bottom lip quivering.

"Gavin my name is Chelsea. You were bitten remember?"

"By Saxon, he's a Werewolf" he nodded in understanding, all his memories returning to him. I offered him a gentle smile, before climbing off his body, and taking a seat next to him. "I'm scared, Chelsea" he sniffed, looking at me with glassy eyes.

"I know you are, Gavin, but you need to keep fighting through it".

He shook his hands, crying some more. "I don't know if I can, I don't know if I want to".

"This is the horrible part, but after this it gets amazing. You have to try and fight for me, Gavin. You have to keep trying". I never got a reply before him, as he began to make odd groaning sounds, and his eyes snapped shut.

I stayed with him for another forty minutes, as he whimpered and groaned in his delirious state. Then things turned from bad, to worse. His heart began to speed up, to an almost wild speed. I called his name, as I shook him slightly, in the hope of arousing him.

But then his heart began to slow down, going the opposite way, to the point where there was a few seconds between each beat. He wasn't going to make it – I knew that right then. "Shit" I screamed angrily. "Saxon".

Saxon was down the stairs in a second. He both looked at Gavin, listened to his slowing heart, and paled. "Grab some shovels, and prepare the car. We'll have to bury him far enough away that--"

"No" Saxon snapped, hands clenching into fists at his side. "He's going to make it. He can't die. He can't".

"Saxon I--" I began but he cut me off.

"He will, Chelsea. Goddammit he will get through it. He will". He began to pace in front of Gavin, entire body rigid with fury and worry. I called his name once more, but he waved me away. Gavin's heart was seconds away from stopping. "I can't let him die".

Saxon suddenly began to remove his clothing, and get down onto all fours. "Why are you Shifting?" I asked nervously.

"If I bite him again, he'll survive the fever, he'll--"

"You can't Force him" I shrieked, heart thumping hard. Saxon was thinking with his heart, not his brain. He hadn't told me a lot about Forced Turns, but what he did tell me, told me that I would have rather died than allowed him to bite me twice.

Forced Turns were violently, and bloodthirsty, and were almost always man-eaters. I gulped, as I looked at Saxon begin his Shift. "No, Saxon, I won't allow you to let this happen".

"Him dying will make this so much worse" Saxon shouted angrily, hands clenching as he pulled his Shift back. "I have to do this, Chels".

"No you don't. You're going to make him into a monster if you do this".

"No, we'll look after him, make sure he doesn't get violent. Just like Dwight, he's part of the Pack and he's a Forced. He can be trained to resist the bloodthirst, just like Dwight and--"

"No, Saxon. It's wrong".

"Stand back Chelsea, I don't want you to get involved".

"Like fuck I won't get involved. I won't let you do this, Saxon. I know that it is scary, but we can get through this. We'll hide his body, and we'll move on tonight. We can make our Pack bigger somewhere else".

"I'm sorry Chelsea, but I have to do this". He paused, guilt in his eyes as he looked at me. "As your Sire, I command you not to stop me doing this". And just like that my tongue held itself. He was using our connection in the most negative way possible – to command. He was in charge, and there wasn't a damn thing I could do about it.

Saxon quickly Shifted, his black Wolf loomed over Gavin's almost dead body. My hands clenched into fists, as every part of me wanted to grab him and stop him. But my body wouldn't move – because my instincts shouted at me to listen to Saxon over every other instinct.

"Ernie" I screamed loudly; the only think I could do. Saxon's eldest brother came running – his feet hitting the floor loudly above us. Saxon growled at me angrily, and I flushed in fear, as he dived at Gavin. I screamed as his teeth sunk into Gavin's wrist.

Ernie barrelled down the stairs, just as Saxon moved away. He looked from his baby brother, to me, to the fresh bite mark on Gavin's wrist and he looked ready to pass out. Saxon had just done the one thing his father, his Dominate, had told him not to do. He had Forced Turned someone. He had Forced Turned a cop.

Chapter Fifteen

Ernie sent Saxon and I back upstairs – and refused to allow us down to help Gavin. Ernie was so angry with his kid brother he instantly sent him out the room, and he told me to keep an eye on him. I could hear Gavin screaming, and calling out for help, and crying like a small kid. I wanted to help Gavin through the change, but Ernie spoke with power – as he was the future Dominate of the Pack – so I listened.

Saxon Shifted back in the lounge, and instantly was at my side trying to take me into his arm. "Don't touch me" I snapped, scooting out of his hold angrily.

"Chelsea?" Saxon asked in confusion – gold specked eyes shining in hurt.

"How could you?" My voice held venom and spite; things I would never had expected to shoot at Saxon at any point. But because of my feelings towards him, his actions hurt me even more.

"I couldn't let him die, Chels. I know it was the wrong choice, but I honestly think we can train him to control himself. I've killed so many people, that I couldn't kill another. And not a cop who could get us in a lot of trouble!"

"You Force Turning Gavin was one thing, but I would have gotten over it. But you commanding me...I don't even know how I'm going to forgive you for that. You know how strongly I feel about you, Saxon, and you abused that. You used our relationship to belittle me and make me feel ridiculous" I snapped, my voice cracking with emotion.

Saxon's big brown eyes looked at me with such hurt, and sorrow, that I instantly wanted to hug him and tell him I forgave him. But I wouldn't, because I was so angry. "I didn't mean to, Chelsea, I swear I didn't. I did it without thinking. I am so fucking sorry".

"It doesn't make a difference" I hissed. "You commanded me, and that really hurt me". I moved over and sat on the couch, as he pulled on some pants and took a seat opposite me. Saxon was quiet for a long while, before he opened his mouth to say something. I silenced him with my hand, and he obeyed.

To keep myself busy while Ernie dealt with Gavin, I first showered and changed before cooking a big stew for lunch. I wasn't the greatest cook, but I had a few of my mother's recipes stored in the back of my head from when I was younger and I helped her.

Gavin went unconscious about two hours later, just as lunch was ready. I took some food down to Ernie, which he gratefully took. Gavin lay naked and unconscious on the floor. "Did he Shift?" I asked.

"Started to, but then he passed out and reverted back" Ernie replied, tucking into the food. I took the tension filled silence as my cue to leave. Ten minutes after I left, Gavin woke up, and the screaming began once more.

I stretched my hearing out, to try and listen to Gavin and Ernie downstairs, but instead I picked something up in the distance. Sirens. "Oh shit" I whispered.

"What? What's wrong?" Saxon demanded, at my side in a second of out worry.

"Listen" I instructed him, he focused on his senses for a moment before he heard what I did. He muttered an oath. "It's coming from the forest southward".

"Where I bit Gavin" Saxon frowned, dark eyes hooded with guilt. I swallowed deeply, before quickly grabbing my boots and my jacket – and pulling them on hastily. "Where are you going?" Saxon demanded.

"To see what I can hear".

"I'm coming too" Saxon stated instantly.

"You've done enough" I snapped angrily. Saxon's eyes shone in hurt, and I instantly felt guilty. But I was still upset with how he had treated me. I brushed past him, determined not to fold at his beautiful gold speckled eyes.

Saxon didn't follow me down to the basement, where Gavin was still screaming. He was half way through a Shift, but it didn't look like he was going any further. His arms and legs were angled the wrong way – with fur and nails – and his spine looked like it was about to break through his body.

Ernie looked up at me as I walked in; his eyes were heavy and drained of all the joy they usually held. "What's wrong?" he asked, still staying knelt down by Gavin.

"Sirens in the forest. I'm going to go take a look" I told him. Ernie frowned deeply, thick worry lines making him look his age for the first time since I'd met him. "Saxon will stay here with you. I just want to listen out for what they are saying".

Ernie nodded, just as Gavin looked up at me – his hazel eyes wild and larger than humanly possible. "Chelsea, help me" he breathed out. I quickly bent in front of him, and softly took his face in my hands. Ernie glanced at me in worry, thinking Gavin may get violent with me. But I wasn't worried.

"You have to keep fighting through it, Gavin. It's going to be hard, but you need to try. For me?" I looked deep into his eyes.

"For you" he breathed out, nodding softly. I offered him a kind smile, as he screamed in pain once more. I moved away from him, and headed over to the door.

"Be careful and stay in human form" Ernie called after me. I nodded at him, as I headed back through the house. Saxon called after me, but I ignored him as I bumped shoulders with him and headed out the front door.

I jogged through the forest, heading south and in the direction of the flashing lights – as the sirens had stopped. I ran for about twenty minutes, before the scent of Gavin's blood filled my sensitive nostrils. I was near where Gavin was bitten by Saxon.

I slowed to a walk, as I heard murmured voices in the distance. "This was where he pressed his panic button" a deep male voice said.

"And there's been no word from Officer Lorraine since?" a female voice replied, the frown in her words obvious. I gulped, when I realised they were talking about Gavin. I eased closer, knowing if I went any further they would see me from where I was.

I thought about it for a moment, before deciding the tree line was the way to go. So springing on my heels, I grabbed a hold of a low hanging branch, and tested the strength of it for a moment. Satisfied it would hold, I pulled myself up.

Swinging myself forward, I landed almost gracefully on the branch – my feet pigeon toed and my arms out to keep my equilibrium, as if I were a gymnast on a balance beam. I was smug for the lightest silence, before pulling myself future up the tree.

I perched near the top, and looked down upon the officers just up to my right. There were four of them; three male officers, and a short female officer. I was sure they couldn't see me, so I carefully took a seat on the branch and listened.

"What was he out here for?" the female asked, making notes in her pocketbook.

"He was called to a domestic assault down the road. But he checked in after dealing with it. Then, about fifteen minutes later, he pressed his panic alarm" the oldest officer answered.

"And where was his radio recovered from?"

"Just up on the left. But there was no signs of a struggle. My best guest would be some sort of animal attack that made him take cover somewhere".

"Alright, we'll let's start by questioning locals with houses around the outskirts of the forest. And if anyone is acting suspicious, report it. At the moment this is just a double check, but if nothing is found by tomorrow morning, then we'll make it a missing person's case".

I didn't listen to anymore, I jumped down from the tree in one leap, landing delicately on the balls of my feet, before taking off towards Ernie's house. We had to move Gavin – because when the police came knocking, they would be able to hear his screams from down the road. This was exactly the kind of mess that Ernie was worried about.

Chapter Sixteen

I ran as fast as I could back to Ernie's house – using my advanced strength to propel me forward. I whipped through the vegetation, rustling leaves in my haste but knowing I was too far away from the cops for them to have heard. My heart was pumping fast. We had to move Gavin before the police came knocking.

When the house came into view, I could see Saxon sitting on the doorstep. He was waiting for me worriedly, with hurt and rejection still in his eyes. I knew what I had said to him was harsh – but what he'd done to me was worse.

He shot to his feet the moment he noticed me running in his direction. As I reached him, his arm went around my waist and pulled me to his chest. Out of habit I leant into him, as he led me back into the house. I didn't want his touch to affect me so much, but it did. It had my heart thumping harder than my run, and my hairs standing up more than a cold night.

"Ernie" I shouted, the moment we stepped inside. Our future Dominate was up the stairs and in front of me in less than a second. "We need to move him. Now!"

"What? Why?"

"He pressed a panic button, some kind of alarm thing to signify he was in trouble and needed assistance. The police said they were going to look through the forests, and search houses around the local area. And those woods are crawling with Wolf tracks, not just from us but from natural Packs. It won't be long before they realise it was a Wolf attack".

Ernie swore, and I nodded in agreement. He ran his hand down his face, a five o clock shadow highlighting his shockingly youthful skin. Saxon's hand gave my waist a squeeze, and even though I was still furious with him it did ease my worry just to know he was next to me.

"We'll move him to a motel, at least then we aren't close enough to the forest for them to look" I suggested, trying to help the situation.

Ernie nodded gravely, "yeah, we'll have to do that". The poor man seemed to have aged twenty years in just the space of a day. I opened my mouth to ask when we would should head out, but before I got the chance, the sound of gravel crunching under tires sounded in my ears. I perked up. "What?" Ernie asked.

"A car is coming down your drive" I told him, and he quickly reached his own hearing out to confirm my words. He cussed colourfully when he realised I was right.

"I'll move Gavin to the car, and we can slip out down the back road behind the car" Saxon offered hastily, heading towards the garage. Ernie grabbed his arm to stop him.

"We moved the car out front when we put Gavin in the garage, remember?"

"Shit".

"Yeah".

"Look, we'll just play it nice and friendly. If they want to look around, we'll quickly show them a few rooms. Gavin is unconscious right?" I asked Ernie, who nodded. "Lock the door, and if they ask what is down there, we'll say we've had a water leak so no one can get down there until we get a man out to fix it".

The car rolled to stop outside, and the doors quickly opened. Boots crunched the gravel, as they headed straight for our door. I took a deep breath, and Ernie and Saxon both swallowed deeply. There was silence, and then the knock came.

Ernie ushered us back into the lounge, where we hid around the corner but could still partially see, as he answered the door. "Hello" Ernie smiled easily, his youthful grin back in place as quickly as it had been lost. Two male officers were in front of him – a tall brunette, and a stocky blonde.

"Good morning, sir, may we come in?" the stocky one asked.

"Of course, of course" he ushered us inside.

"My name is Officer Tobin and this is Officer Hewitt" the tall one explained, and Ernie smiled brightly at both of them.

"Ernest Henderson, but please call me Ernie".

"Mr Henderson, is there anyone else at this address at the moment?" Officer Tobin questioned.

"My baby brother and his girlfriend are visiting. I'll just get them". We let Ernie walk into the lounge, before we followed him out without a word. "Kids this is Officer Tobin and Officer Hewitt. Officer's this is my kid brother, Saxon, and his girlfriend Chelsea Russell" Ernie introduced us.

"Are all three of you residence in this house?" Tobin asked.

"No, Chelsea and I live in Toronto together" Saxon replied, hand slipping around my waist.

"Canadian eh? I have an uncle who lives in Montreal, always telling me how much better it is than the US. Can't say I agree though" Hewitt laughed, "what do you do, son?"

"I'm a PI".

Hewitt laughed, "a private investigator hey? You lot make my job awful, always getting into crooks that we can't, making us look incompetent". He gave another hearty laugh. "What about you, Miss Russell, what do you do?"

"In between jobs at the moment" I replied with a small uneasy smile.

"What about you, Mr Henderson?" Tobin asked, more serious than his partner.

"I'm a professor of anthropology" Ernie replied. "Sorry, Officers, I don't mean to be rude. But what is this all about?"

"We're just doing a basic scale of the area, after one of our Officers is missing. We just need to talk to all people in a five mile radius to the forest he last reported from".

"I hope he's alright" I said, hoping I sounded convincing. I was pretty sure I did, as Hewitt gave a small nod of agreement.

"So do we, Miss Russell".

"Mr Henderson, do you mind if we have a quick look around? Just to make sure, you're welcome to decline of course – we haven't got a warrant – we just want to tick you off our list".

Ernie nodded softly, "of course, Saxon and I will give you a tour. Chelsea, why don't you put some tea on?"

I held my tongue at the sexist dismissal, but knew it wasn't because I was a women, but because if shit went down Gavin trusted me and would leave with me more than the other two. So even though I didn't want to make tea, I knew that I had to stay separate from the officers.

Ernie and Saxon showed the officers around the house, as I made tea – my ears and mind miles away from the boiling kettle. Just as I the kettle began to whistle, I noise reached my ears. A groan of pain, and it was coming from below. Gavin was waking up.

"Shit" I hissed, as I turned the gas down. "Saxon if you hear me, cough" I whispered. There was silence for a moment, before Saxon coughed as Ernie carried on talking to the officers. "Gavin is waking up. I'm going down to the basement, try and get them out as quickly as possible. Cough again if you understand". A moment of pause, then another cough.

I slipped out of the kitchen, and silently scurried around the landing. I eased the basement door open, making sure to pull it slowly so it didn't creak, before heading through. I gently closed the door behind me, as Gavin groaned louder.

I raced down the rickety stairs, on light tread, and practically dived on top of Gavin. He was rising on the mattress; eyes wild and his lips turned up in a snarl. He looked feral, more Wolf than human.

I pushed him back onto his back, and he snarled at me – his teeth snapping like a wild dog with rabies. I pinned his body with mine, as I used my strength to hold him down as the thrashing began, and my left hand clamped over his mouth.

He tried to push me off with his hands, and I quickly grabbed both of his wrists with my right hand, and held them above his head. It was like a horror movie, I was the priest and Gavin was the possessed man. But in this version, I was the one with super strength. However, Gavin kept fighting and it was hard to keep him still.

"What's through here?" Tobin asked, just outside the door and I mentally swore.

"The basement" Saxon replied, and I heard the handle turn.

"Why is it locked?"

"Because it flooded last week, and we're trying to dry it out while we wait for the man to come look at the pipes"

Ernie lied smoothly. There was a moment, as my Pack brothers and I held our breaths.

"Alright, no problem" Hewitt finally said, and I heavily exhaled.

"Where's your girlfriend gone?" Tobin questioned and I cussed again. There was a silence, as I held Gavin to the ground. "Mr Henderson, where is your girlfriend?" Again more silence. "Mr Henderson, I am only going to ask you once more, where is your girlfriend?"

"I don't know, Officer, I was upstairs with you" Saxon replied, as I whipped my head around the basement as I looked for something to bind Gavin with. I quickly saw duct tape – but it was on the other side of the basement, on top of a packing box. I'd have to let go of Gavin to get it.

"Why would she leave the kettle on the gas, Mr Henderson?" Tobin demanded, and I knew I had to go back up there. As Saxon bullshitted some kind of answer, I took a deep breath of courage. Letting go of Gavin, I dived across the room.

Gavin was shocked with my sudden movement, and for a second was confused, before he gave a piercing screamed. "What the hell was that?" Hewitt demanded. My hands sealed around the tape, but as I turned back around in haste, my feet kicked a tub of yellow paint it went flying. It splashed up me, but I didn't pause for a moment.

I dived back on Gavin and taped his mouth first. He shrieked into the make-shift gag, as I struggled to tape up his limb. "Mr Henderson, we need to see what is going on down in the basement" Tobin snapped.

"You can't" Ernie replied – panic obvious in his voice. Tobin and Ernie began to argue, as I finally managed to wrap the tape around his wrists. I gave myself a mental high-five, before diving on his legs, and taping them together; which was easier since he could no long hit me.

Once they were connected, I flipped Gavin onto front and then taped his wrists and legs together so he couldn't get up. And then, as the voices reached the door, I jumped off Gavin and sprinted up the stairs. Just as Tobin turned the handle, I pushed the door open.

"Oh sorry" I smiled, trying to contain my laboured breathing.

"Miss Russell what was going on down there?"

"Oh we have a problem with the water pipes, and I could still smell the damp. So I went down to make sure there was no mould, but I saw a rat! I freaked and accidently knocked paint over myself. I'm surprised you didn't hear me, I screamed the place down".

"We did here you, Miss Russel, we were concerned" Hewitt replied, offering me a small smile as he looked at the yellow paint that covered my jeans.

"Well, I think we can safely say we're satisfied" Tobin said, "we'll leave you all to get on with your afternoon".

Chapter Seventeen

The moment we closed the door on the cops, Saxon practically attacked me. I gave a yelp of shock, as he pounced on me, his arms holding me in an almost aggressive hug. His firm body pressed tightly to mine, as his hands held me in a tight grip – that told me he didn't plan to let me go any time soon.

"I heard the scream and I thought it was you. I thought he'd hurt you" he whispered into my neck, as I relaxed into the embrace and buried my own face into his neck. His scent was amazing; filling my senses, and sending euphoria throughout my entire body. I heard Ernie slip out the room, obviously to give us some privacy, and I was glad.

My arms lifted automatically and wrapped around his neck, as I got as close as I could. "I am so sorry, Chelsea, so fucking sorry. I am so ashamed of myself, for both Force Turning Gavin and commanding you. You know me Chelsea, you know I'm not like that. You know me, you know me better than anyone. I don't know how much longer I can last with you angry with me".

"It's hasn't even been a day, Saxon".

"And even that's too long for me".

"You really hurt me" I whispered, my face still firmly pressed against the soft skin of his nape.

"I know, I fucked up so bad. I betrayed your trust, and our bond. It's just, I'm the youngest in the family so most of my brothers had moved out by the time I got to about thirteen, and I don't really have anyone I would class as a friend. Yet, I met you and everything in my life seemed to brighten up. You're the only person in my life that I can truly open up to. And I can't lose you because I was a dick".

"A colossal dick" I corrected him.

He gave a soft chuckle, which fanned over my neck and made me shiver. "Fine, yes, a colossal dick. Forgive me?"

"You're not forgiven, but I'm not angry anymore". I pulled away slightly, but he kept his arms tightly around me. I faces were inches apart, and my breath quicken of its own accord. I looked into those beautiful brown, gold speckled, eyes of Saxon and I melted slightly. His pupils dilated slightly.

All I wanted to do was kiss him, and show him exactly what I felt for him. Our noses brushed, and our breathing mixed together. My heart was thumping almost as hard as his, and I knew that I wasn't the only way feeling the sexual attraction between us. There had always been animal connection, just like I felt with Ernie, but there was definitive sexual connection in that moment.

Saxon's eyes snapped shut, and mine quickly followed. We both leant in and—

"Get away from me" Gavin screamed, and we jumped apart quicker than I thought I could move. I blushed softly, as did Saxon, as what we were about to do set in.

"Guys, I hate to interrupt, but we need to move him" Ernie called from the hallway. Saxon and I quickly composed ourselves and rushed out to Ernie. Together we all headed down to the basement. "Shit, remind me to never piss you off" Ernie muttered as he looked at Gavin's restraints and how no matter how hard he fought, they weren't giving any.

"I was in Brownies" I shrugged.

"Brownies?" Saxon questioned.

"British equivalent of Girl Scouts, but they don't sell cookies" I explained.

"When did you get your bondage and torture badge?" Ernie teased me, and I gave a small laugh. He bent down next to Gavin, who snarled at him – his eyes large and black, showing him to be more Wolf than human.

"Should we really move him?" Saxon questioned, as Gavin tried to snap at him. "I just mean, it can't be long until he Shifts now, and surely him screaming in a motel will draw more attention. We were only going to move him because of the cops, but is there any point now?"

Ernie and I were silent for a moment, before his brother nodded. "You're right, we might as well keep him here. It's getting late, hopefully he'll Shift at some point tonight".

"I'll stay with him tonight" Saxon spoke up, Ernie opened his mouth to argue. "I made this mess, I have to deal with it. I really am sorry, Ernest, I was just scared".

Ernie sighed heavily, "I know you are, pup. But you know at some point you have to tell Dad, and that is when shit will hit the fan". He clasped his baby brother's shoulder, and I knew that Ernie felt the same as me towards Saxon. He was no longer angry, but Saxon was not forgiven.

Ernie pulled a twenty from his back pocket, and handed it to me. "Go pick us up something for dinner. We haven't gotten anything in" he said. I took the money, before heading back up to main house. I knew Ernie asked me because I was the youngest Wolf, so was classed as the Omega because I was the most inexperience, but I really wanted to stay with them.

I quickly changed, throwing my paint-stained jeans away, before taking Saxon's car into the nearest town. I cussed in annoyance, when I realised there was some kind of fundraiser going on in the main part of the town, so I couldn't drive through.

I growled as I went the long way around, and parked the car behind a large abandoned building as I couldn't be bother to drive through all the other diverted traffic. As I got out the car, I heard movement and looked up to see a man on top of the building. Thinking nothing of it, I walked into the main town and picked up a pizza. But when I returned, he was still standing up there.

Curiosity killed the cat, but I was a Wolf so I decided to head up there. The stairs inside were rickety and metal, and my boots clicked on them slightly as I walked up them. It took me about ten minutes to reach the top of the abandoned building – that due to the rusty machinery told me it used to be some kind of saw mill or factory.

When I reached the roof, the metal door had been propped open with a brown satchel, that obviously belonged to the man standing on the edge of the roof – his hand resting on the small wall around the edge.

I stepped over the satchel, and waited for a few moments. "You can do this, Landon, just fucking jump" the man muttered to himself. From behind I couldn't see much of his features, but I could see the smoothness of his black skin, and the smart cut of his dark hair. He was short, an inch or so over my five foot five.

"No one will miss you, Landon, so just get it over with" he carried on talking to himself.

"You know I'm pretty sure you have to be standing *on* the wall, to jump off it" I commented, and the man – Landon – yelped in shock. He span around to face me, large brown eyes wide and scared. His face was smooth, and almost baby like, with large oval eyes and large lips.

"How the hell did you get up here?" Landon snapped, looking at me with annoyance – but there also a small blush on his dark skin, to show he was embarrassed with the fact I had found him at possibly the lowest point in his life.

"There is this amazing thing called stairs. Great invention really" I replied sarcastically.

"I wasn't going to jump. I was just seeing the view" he lied.

"Before or after you gave yourself the little pep talk to end your life?" I moved closer to him, as he turned away from me and looked out at the lights of the small town in front of him. The sun was practically gone, with just the small red glow of dusk in the distance.

"I have nothing left to live for. I would be doing people a favour by killing myself" Landon stated, no bitterness in his voice just simple fact. It saddened me to meet a man so low and depressed, that he didn't think there was anything left to keep him alive. He looked to be about Saxon's age, give or take a few years, but still too young to feel like that.

"How old are you, Landon?" I questioned, as I leant against the small wall where he was.

"Twenty seven".

"You still have a good seventy years left, and you're going to throw that all away because you're feeling a little down today?" I asked.

"I've been coming up here every night for the past two weeks".

"Yet you come down and go home every night".

"Yeah". He gave a large sigh, running a hand down his face. "Why do you care?" His words weren't horrible, just inquisitive – as if he didn't know why some stranger would want to help a stranger about to kill himself.

"You ever wanted to be a different person Landon? A different person, with a different life, in a different state, with a new family who loves everything about you?" I questioned him suddenly.

"If you don't want a sarcastic answer, then don't ask stupid questions" he replied with an eye roll. I chuckled softly.

"Alright, so you want all those things. What if I could give you those things?"

Landon glanced my way, "you're very beautiful. But I'm at least seventy two percent sure I'm gay".

"Only seventy two percent?"

"I still find myself stealing glances at boobs. But I have yet to work out if that is just out of habit".

"I see" I smirked, already deciding I liked Landon. "Well I wasn't offering a romance. I was offering the chance to become a Werewolf". There was a pause as Landon looked at me, before he let out a small laugh.

"A Werewolf huh?" he asked, trying to keep a straight face. I nodded, keeping my serious look on my face although I wanted to laugh – as I knew exactly what he was thinking about. "So if you're a Werewolf, how come you're wearing a silver necklace?" he mused.

I gave a small laugh, before smiling at him. Moving quickly, I vaulted myself over the small wall on the roof, and threw myself over the edge of the building. Landon yelped in shock, and I soared towards the ground.

I landed next to my car, with my feet planted apart and my body in crouch. I had landed a lot better than I had thought. I straightened up, and looked up at Landon – who was leaning over the edge of the large building in shock.

"Are you coming down?" I shouted up to him. "I have a pizza in the car that's going cold, and the two grown Wolves I have at home will be getting very hungry now. So if you don't get a move on, you'll be next on the menu".

Chapter Eighteen

"I'm home, and I brought a stray with me" I shouted, as I headed back into the house with Landon trailing behind me. Saxon and Ernie came up the stairs, and pause when they noticed the small man at my heels.

"Chelsea?" Saxon questioned, as I placed the pizza down in the lounge.

"Saxon, this is Landon, he's going to be our new Turn. Landon, this is Saxon, he's going to be the one who bites you" I replied, and the brothers exchanged looks of shock.

"Hi" Landon smiled shyly at them. "Chelsea explained that we had to wait until the dangerous Turn was better until you bit me. But she brought me with her anyway".

"Forced Turn" I corrected him, and he nodded in agreement.

"You can't just bring humans home" Ernie snapped at me in annoyance.

"Don't speak to her like that" Saxon barked at his brother, and Landon looked confused. "Look, we're building the Pack up. And Chelsea is just helping me out with that". Walking over his arms slipped around my waist, and I automatically leant into his side. He turned away from his brother and to Landon. "Saxon" he introduced himself, smiling.

Landon shook the hand that Saxon stretched out to him, before all of us headed into the lounge. Ernie took two slices of the pizza, and headed back down with Gavin, leaving the three of us together.

We all tucked into the pizza, as Landon questioned Saxon on everything related to Werewolves. And just like he had done with me, Saxon answered each questioned patiently and in as much detail as he could.

"I was thinking Sax" I whispered, moving so I pressed so close to Saxon that I was practically sitting on his lap. But he didn't seem to mind, he just slipped his arms around me and held me as close as possible. "We only have two more weeks before your dad wants us back at the territory. Maybe you should bite Landon, and I'll get him through the change in a motel. That way you and Ernie can deal with Gavin and then we can move on as soon as we can".

Saxon thought about it for a moment, his face inches from mine. I could have leant in and kissed him, but I held myself, no matter how much my body reacted from having him so close to him. But for that moment I just enjoyed having his scent surrounding my body and relaxing me.

"I don't want you to get hurt" he frowned. "It was just earlier, when Gavin screamed, I kept thinking how unpredictable the fever and the change is that--"

"I'm not a kid, Saxon. I'll be fine, I promise" I gave him a small smile, before squeezing his thigh in reassurance. He sighed heavily, but nodded in agreement.

"Yeah, we've been here too long. We need to wrap things up and move on before we make life for Ernie even harder" he said. I gave him a look. "Alright before *I* make life for Ernie even harder".

"I just think it might be the best way to handle the situation" I nodded, and Saxon pressed a kiss on my cheek. I quickly packed a bag, before checking on Ernie and Gavin. Luckily, Gavin was going through the first Shift, so it wouldn't be too much longer until he was somewhat back to normal – or so we hoped.

"Are you alright?" I asked Landon, when I returned to him and Saxon in the lounge. They both stood up to greet me, and Saxon's arms went around me again.

"I'm scared" he admitted, "excited as well. But scared".

"That's understandable" Saxon nodded, "it's not exactly an everyday occurrence. I'll bite you now, and then Chelsea will take you somewhere safe to help you through the transformation. If you survive, you will be our brother and you will have the life you always wanted".

"So I'll automatically become a billionaire after you bite me?" Landon joked.

"I wish" I snorted, as Saxon laughed. Saxon turned to me, and nodded me out the room softly. Landon understood to hang back and give us some privacy as we slipped outside the room.

"Be careful, and if he doesn't survive, don't bury him alone. Call me about anything. Anything at all" Saxon told me, cupping my face with his cheeks. I relaxed into his hold, my eyes closing for a brief moment to enjoy being with him. I wanted him to hold me forever.

"After this is all over, will you promise me we'll just spend a day together? Just me and you?" I questioned. Saxon smiled and rested his forehead against mine.

"I can't wait until I can just be with you again. When this is all over, I promise to take you someplace quiet and just be with you and no one else".

"You promise?" My heart was beating out of my chest.

"I promise" Saxon replied, pressing another kiss to my cheek. "Right, we'd better make sure you get Landon to a motel before it gets too late to find a place". We pulled away, and headed back into the lounge.

"Ready?" I asked Landon, who nodded yes. Saxon took a deep breath before Shifting – Landon watched in fascination, with a small bit of fear. When Saxon was full Shifted, he quickly rubbed his side against me to show his affection. I couldn't help but blush at his demonstration, even though it wasn't in a sexual way.

Landon shakily held his wrist out to the large Wolf in front of him. He yelped in shock when Saxon nipped his skin. A little bit of blood welled up, which I quickly wiped away with a damp cloth before wrapping it up with a thick bandage.

I pressed a kiss to Saxon's fur, and he growled happily before I huddled a slightly stunned Landon into the car. I drove to a motel that Landon knew, a few miles outside of the town we had met. I brought a room in cash and under a fake name.

"I'm breaking a sweat" Landon complained, as we got into the shitty room. Walking over to him, I pressed the back of my hand on his forehead.

"You're running a fever. Take your clothes off, I'll run you a bath" I told him. Landon paused as he glanced at his clothing nervously. "Nakedness is only a problem for humans, Landon. I don't see nakedness the same way anymore. So don't worry, it won't do anything for me".

"Don't say that before you actually see me naked. People with stronger wills than you have crumpled at the sight of me shirtless".

"I'm sure" I replied sarcastically. I heard him laughing as I headed into the bathroom, turning the rusty taps on in the bath. Cold water sputtered out, and I poured in the bucket of ice I had taken from the lobby. Once the water reached the top, I turned it off and called Landon in. He didn't enter.

I poked my head back into the bedroom, to see Landon leaning against the wall. "Hey, you alright?" I rushed to his side. He had taken his clothing off, and I could see the layer of thick sweat coating his skin.

"I went dizzy for a moment there" he breathed out.

"Come on, the bath is cold". I took his hand and pulled him after me. He stumbled with a groan, as his feet dragged after him. I helped him into the bath, before opening the windows above the bath for a little cold air. I was cold, but I didn't complain any.

I got Landon a cold glass of water, and forced him to drink it. Then I pulled a chair up next to the bath, and sat with Landon as he tried to get his temperature down. "Feeling any better?" I asked him, after a few moments.

He didn't reply, so I moved forward and shook his shoulders gently. He didn't say anything, but his eyes were fluttering left and right as if he were watching something on a TV. I settled back down in my seat – knowing he was having a vision of something. I thought back to my own fever and shivered on his behalf.

Landon began by making choking noises, but he was not choking, before he began to thrash manically. I cussed when he went under the water, and I quickly jumped out of my chair and grabbed his body. He fought against me, but my strength allowed me to hold him upright.

He carried on fighting, and trying to get out of my grip, for about twenty minutes; and it didn't look like he was calming down any time soon. I quickly stripped my clothing off, before jumping into the bath with him. I sat behind him, with his body lying on mine – something I had done with many boyfriends, but had never been the one being leant on.

My arms wrapped around his body, and I held him still as he fought. I thought about Saxon as I sat there, I couldn't help myself. I knew I shouldn't have read much into his comments to take me away for a weekend, but I just couldn't help myself.

No one had truly cared for me since my parents, and that was why I had such issues with men. I always fell in love too quickly. I was so desperate for someone to take care of me, and love me, and want to be with me; that I seemed to find myself alone as I drove too many people away with my incisive need to feel wanted. I was very independent, but I just craved someone to love me.

And then, along came Saxon. A man who cared, who looked after me like no one had in years, and all he wanted was to be with me. He would touch me, or hug me, or kiss me whenever he could and never made it seem like it was a hindrance – and I felt so wanted and needed, that I couldn't help but fall in love with him.

Every time I saw him, my heart beat a bit faster. Every time I touched him, electricity shot through my body. Every time I thought of him being hurt, I felt sick and wanted to be as close to him as I could. All I wanted to do was be with him, and touch him, and kiss him and tell him I loved him. But I couldn't, because I didn't want to risk our friendship if he didn't feel the same back. But, fuck, I wanted so badly for him to feel the same.

"Chelsea?" Landon groaned, snapping me out of my thoughts. I suddenly realised I was holding him tightly but he was not actually fighting anymore. I eased my hold.

"Yeah it's me" I whispered into his ear, as he leant back into me – his head resting on my shoulder.

"I can't tell if this is turning me on or not" he said, and I huffed a laugh out.

"I thought you were gay?"

"I told you I hadn't decided yet. But I can tell you wholeheartedly that I am so cold that my balls are so far inside my body, that soon they're going to come out my fucking mouth". He shivered, but he was also still sweating. Before I could answer, or laugh, Landon back's arched and he screamed.

I heard his spine snap, and then his bones reset. A second late it snapped once more, before resetting back the way it was before. "What the hell was that?" Landon whimpered, obviously scared.

"You've survived the fever, now you just have to get through the Shift".

Chapter Nineteen

"You're black" I stated, running my hands through his fur. Landon gave me look, which he didn't need a voice box to say – 'no shit Sherlock'. "I meant your fur, shit head" I told him, chuckling at my newest Pack member.

Landon's Shift was a lot slower than mine, because he kept fighting it. No matter how many times I tried to get him to relax, he just kept seizing up in fear. He didn't like the pain, not that I could really blame him, so had tried to fight the Shift off. But after thirty minutes, the Shift won out.

"I can't wait to tell Saxon you survived, he's going to be so happy" I smiled at Landon. He huffed out, as his large black eyes sparkled in the motel light. He was sat on the floor, his paws crossed, and his large head rested on my legs. My fingers were stroking through his fur, and with the way his ears pinned back and he made soft growling noises, I could tell that he liked it.

I glanced at the digital clock on the old fashioned TV, and even though it was three in the morning, I was hungry. And I knew that Landon would be starving when he Shifted back. "I'm going out to get food. Can you Shift back while I'm out?" My fingers ran down his back.

Landon's head gave a small nod, and I smiled, before standing up and moving away from him. I was still naked, but Landon – and his new instincts – didn't even seem to notice. Nude forms were no longer a concern to him; which was exactly how he should be.

I bent down and pressed a kiss to the side of Landon's head. He growled, before playfully diving backwards. I laughed, as he bounced on the balls of his feet, with a mischievous look on his face. I grabbed my clothing, and began to redress – Landon nudged me with his wet nose as I pulled my jeans on.

"Stop it, dick" I laughed, I could see he wanted to play. "I'll take you for a run tomorrow, and we can play. Alright?" I smiled, ruffling his fur. He huffed in agreement, before rubbing his side against me to show his affection. I quickly pulled my sweater on, followed by my boots. I pressed another kiss to Landon's head. "Shift while I'm away" I ordered him.

I took Saxon's car, and used his hands free to call him. "Chelsea, is everything alright?" he answered instantly – his voice heavy with fatigue.

"I'm fine. Sorry, did I wake you?"

"It doesn't matter. Are you sure there is nothing wrong?" he asked. Once more my heart soared, and I fell a little bit more in love with him – simply because he cared.

"Landon survived" I told him with a bright smile. There was a pause on the phone, but I could tell from Saxon's sharp intake of breath that he was still there.

"Landon made it through?" he asked in disbelief; voice full of child-like glee.

"Yeah, he's Shifting back now as I grab some food" I replied, grinning myself.

"Thank god, I was getting worried no one would ever survive. I'm so glad. Should I come meet you?"

"No, no. You stay with Gavin. How is he doing?"

"Not good" Saxon sighed, voice no longer full of happiness. "I fucked up so bad, Chels. Honestly, I don't know what to do".

"There is nothing you can do now, Sax. Just wait it out, and hope we can get him back".

"I've ruined his life, Chels. How can I ever live with that?" His voice was thick with emotions, and it made a lump form in my throat. I wanted to badly to have him in my arms.

"Maybe you did ruin it" I replied truthfully – I could never lie to Saxon. "But you have also given a lot people better lives, Saxon. Landon and I, we are both finally happy. Something neither of us have had in a long time".

"I hadn't been happy in a long time either" he stated, voice barley a whisper. "But I'm happy whenever I am with you".

"I'm happy whenever I am with you, too". There was a heavy since between us, both of us just listening to the other's soft breathing. I was the one to break the silence, as I turned into a fast food restaurant. "I have to go now, Saxon. But Landon and I will be back in the morning".

"If you need anything, find me".

"Always" I replied, smiling, before hanging up.

It was quiet inside the fast food restaurant, just a few people dotted around eating. Two people were behind the counter, chatting and drinking strong coffee. Both were men, and both looked up when I walked in. They lowered their voices, but of course I could still hear them.

"Fuck, dude, look at her" one of them whispered.

"Rock, paper, scissors for who gets to serve her" the other hissed. Their hands moved, and the second man won. The first one cussed, before childishly sulking as I reached the counter. The second guy grinned flirtatiously at me.

"Hey, beautiful, what can I get ya?"

"Eighteen burgers, all with fries and two cokes" I told him with a small smile.

"Wow, that's a lot of food" the man replied, as the other man dishonoured their pact and walked over anyway.

"All my friends have the munchies" I replied, and the man laughed. As he went to get my large order, the other man stayed and flirted pointless with me for a moment. I smiled, and answered, but didn't show any interest. After I paid, and left the restaurant, I heard the door open after me.

I slowed my walk, as I strode across the deserted lot, towards my car. Someone followed me – their footsteps speeding up as they raced in my direction. Taking a deep inhale of the scent, I knew it was just one of the men who was sitting in the restaurant eating alone.

I walked even slower, to make sure that he caught up. When I reached my car, I placed the food in the car, as the footsteps reached me. I spun quickly, to become faced with a tall man with a short beard and a shaggy hair. I opened my mouth, to demand to know what he wanted, when he dived at me.

His human speed was nothing compared to mine, and I scooted to the side so fast I was like a blur. He tripped as he hit into the passenger's side of car, his hands crashing into Saxon's door and making a dent. I was annoyed more about that, than the unprovoked attack.

He turned around to face me, with both disbelief and annoyance in his face. Disbelief at my quick movement, and annoyance at me putting up a fight. Digging into his pocket, he pulled a small pen knife out of his pocket. I sighed deeply.

Sarcastically, I put my hands in the air. "Oh no. A pathetically small knife. Please, oh, please don't kill me" I said, in a monotonic voice to show just how stupid I thought he was being.

"Shut up bitch".

"A bitch? How original" I rolled my eyes at him. He dived at me again, and I met him with a kick. My leg shot out, making contact with his wrist and knocking the knife from his hand. He cussed, as it flew into the night.

Jumping forward, I grabbed a handful of his shirt and pushed him up against Saxon's car. My inhuman strength made his eyes bulge. "Let's put it like this, asshole. This is a little warning. Next time you decide to approach a women, or a man, hell, even if you threaten an animal, I will make sure it is the last fucking thing you do". He opened his mouth to speak, so I gripped harder and his feet lifted off the ground. He quickly shut up.

I glared at him for a heavy second, before dropped him. Just to get my point across, I gave him a quick kick in his crowned jewels. He yelled in shock, as he grabbed his crotch, before sprinting off into the night. I flipped his retreating back the bird.

Back at the motel, I found Landon entering the last stage of his Shift. So I gently shut the door, before taking a seat on the floor next to him. He screamed into clenched teeth, as his back arched before his spine realigned.

When he finished, his dark skin was covered in sweat. "Hey" he breathed out, on his hands and knees as he looked up at me. "That hurt like a bitch". His breath was fast and laboured, as he rested his head against the floor as he regained his composure. I ran a hand over his skin, and he shivered softly.

"Go shower. I have dinner ready" I smiled, leaning down and pressing a kiss to his shoulder. He nodded, before slowly getting to his feet – cringing as he did so. Landon quickly showered, and pulled a pair of boxers on, before we both climbed into the bed together.

"I have never been so hungry in my entire life" he said, through a mouthful of his burger. I laughed, as I bit into one myself. I grabbed my phone, and took a picture of Landon and I eating the massive pile of fast food in the bed, and sent it to Saxon. He didn't reply, but I assumed he was asleep.

"I can't believe I'm actually a Werewolf" Landon laughed, after we polished off all the burgers. He ate eleven of them, and I ate seven of them – before we shared the fries between us.

"I still can't believe it either. Crazy huh?" I chuckled, and he smiled. I glanced at the clock, seeing that it was almost five in the morning. "We should get some sleep. I'll set the alarm for nine" I told him.

Landon threw all the rubbish in the bin, as I set the alarm. We both then slipped under the covers, my body instantly curling into Landon. "This doesn't feel weird, but maybe it should" he muttered, as his arms wrapped around my waist.

"Don't question your instincts" I whispered into his ear – the same thing Saxon had told me. "You're not human anymore, Landon. We don't think of nakedness, or touching as taboo. We're Wolves now, Landon, and you have to let your mind act like one".

"So Saxon won't get jealous because I'm in bed with you?" he asked.

"Of course not" I replied. But what I really meant was; 'I wish'.

Chapter Twenty

When I woke up, Landon was snoring softly next to me. I smiled brightly at him for a few minutes, noticing the differences in his appearance since his Shift. His cheekbones were more prominent, the beginning of a six pack starting on his once slim stomach, his shoulders larger and stronger. He was never ugly, but he would definitely have more attention with his new looks.

I flicked the alarm off, deciding I would allow Landon a few more minutes sleep as I showered. The water from the cheap motel shower took a while to warm up, so I moved my feet together for a moment before stepping under the lukewarm spray.

"How's the water?" Landon asked from behind me. I jumped in shock, spinning around in the shower to see him entering the bathroom. He yawned largely, running a hand over his face as he shuffled in. I was so deep into thought – of course about Saxon – that I had allowed him to get the jump on me. I shook myself, quickly recovering.

"Not very warm" I replied, as I rubbed the soap over me. Landon mumbled incoherent morning babble, before taking his boxers off and stepping into the shower with me. I quickly realised he was not a morning person, so we showered in silence.

After losing his job two months earlier, Landon had moved back in with his parents. So, we decided to pick up his supplies before heading back to Ernie's. Landon offered to drive, simply because he liked Saxon's car and wanted to show off to the people in his neighbourhood that he was driving a Mercedes.

"I'm sorry" Landon muttered, embarrassed, as we turned onto his road.

"Why?"

"It's a bit shitty around these parts".

"Before Saxon found me, I was a stripper who would have loved to live in a place like this" I told him bluntly. "You don't have to pretend to be anyone you're not Landon. And never apologise for where you come from".

Landon ran into his parent's house to pack a bag, and I waited in the car. After about ten minutes, a group of four men walked down the street – all heading for Landon's house. I got out the car quietly, and leant against the door as they reached me.

"That's a nice car you've got there" the man at the front said. He was tall, dark features, and a lean body.

"It's my boyfriends" I replied flippantly.

"You must have a rich boyfriend" he stated, as his friends shared looks. Before I could reply, Landon came out his front door with a bag slung over his back. He skidded to a stop when he saw the men in front of him. "Landon" the man called, as his friends all nodded at my Pack brother.

"John, guys" Landon nodded, jaw setting as he bit down. He quickly walked over to me, standing almost in front of me to block the men from me. "How are you?"

"Good" John nodded, eyeing Landon and I closely. I took the bag off Landon's back, and threw it into the car. "You off somewhere?"

"Just out of town for a while" Landon replied, smile strained. Taking my arm, he practically pushed me into the car. I wasn't happy, but I didn't fight him either. The men all frowned deeply, exchanged another look, before watching Landon jump into the driver's side and speed off.

"Want to explain what that was about?" I asked, frowning.

"I needed a bit of extra cash a few months ago, for my mum's medication. So I borrowed some from a family friend. Well, not so much a family friend, as the local drug dealer who used to sell my sister coke. However, when I couldn't pay it back, he made be pay the debt back in a different way".

"Running drugs?" I asked.

"What? No, nothing that extreme. Just doing a few errands and things, to help him out. But now that I'm leaving, with this unpaid debt, well let's just say he won't be happy" Landon sighed. I nodded slowly in understanding – being able to tell he didn't want to talk about it.

Back at Ernie's house, Saxon instantly embraced Landon. I smiled at the two, as they clasped backs and smiled. I pressed a kiss to Ernie's cheek, before hugging Saxon when Landon moved away. "I missed you last night" he whispered into my ear, sending shivers down my spine.

"I missed you too" I replied, as he kissed my cheek – his lips lingering longer than necessary. Not that I was complaining any. When we pulled away, his hand stayed around my waist and I leant into his side. "How's Gavin?"

"Sleeping" Ernie sighed, "he's remembers everything, and he seems alright. A bit scared and jumpy. But not much else".

"He was asking for you" Saxon told me, giving my waist a squeeze.

"I'll make sure I'm there when he wakes up" I stated, offering him a small smile. We all headed through to the lounge, where we all sat down – Saxon and Landon cuddling on either side of me. It felt nice to have them both their; my two Pack brothers.

Saxon, Landon and I spoke for a few hours; mostly telling Landon everything he needed to know. Then Ernie made us lunch, before he and Saxon made a run into town to get more food and see if they could hear any gossip about Gavin's disappearance in the local town.

"You look tired" I said to Landon, once they left. I ran my finger under his dark eyes.

"I feel it" he grumbled, stifling a yawn. "My body in still exhausted from the Shift and the fever".

"Why don't you go and get a few hours' sleep now?" I asked, as I headed upstairs to check on Gavin. Landon followed, hesitation of the proposal obvious from the small hum that came out of his mouth in order to give his excuses a moment to surface.

"Hmm. Maybe later, don't want to miss anything cool while I'm sleeping". He shot me a bright smile, and I chuckled at him in turn. When I reached the top of the stairs, I paused and listened to Gavin's breathing – it was soft and even. He was still sleeping.

"You head back downstairs and make some tea. I'm just going to make sure he's alright" I told Landon, who instantly obeyed. It felt different with Landon than with the others, because he was a lower rank than me. Saxon told me that the rank positions are based on the age of a person's Wolf life – unless the Dominate hired their ranking.

Saxon used to be lowest rank in the Pack; as out of all the remaining Pack members, he was the last person to Shift due to him being the youngest of the Dominates kids. However, after he bit me – and I became the most recent Shift, I had become the lowest rank – the Omega of the Pack. But, suddenly, Landon was below me and his instincts were to obey me as I was above him in the pecking order.

Gavin was also below me, but I wasn't sure how that would work out. The Forced Shift would mean that his instincts are different to that of a normal Werewolf who was either Born or Turned. So, I didn't know what that meant for his rank.

I pushed the door to the spare room open softly; the creak of the hinges only small but enough to wake. I cringed, as I poked my head through the small gap between the door and frame. Gavin lay on the bed, eyes open and blankly staring up at the spinning ceiling fan above him.

Seeing he was awake, I eased the door the rest of the way and stepped in. He didn't turn to face me, which I took as a bad sign. Frowning, I shut the door, before cautiously walking over to the bed.

"Gavin? Are you alright?" I questioned. The tremor in my voice was obvious.

"Why are you scared of me, Chelsea?" he demanded, eyes not moving from their emotionless stare.

"I'm not scared of you, Gavin".

"Your heart rate just changed, that means you're lying" he stated, and I bit my lip because there was no way I could fight him on the point – I couldn't change my heart beat to make it seem like I was telling the truth. So I would just have to stretch the truth as far as I could, to ensure that I kept Gavin as complacent as possible.

"Saxon is scared of me too. And the other one, the elder brother" he added.

"Ernest" I informed him.

"Hmm. Yes, him. You are all scared of me, yet you made me this way. You made me a monster".

"You are not a monster, Gavin" I gushed fiercely, rushing to his bed side and reaching for his limp hand. As soon as my skin touched his, he jerked his hand away at lightning speed, and sat up. Finally, his eyes met mine. Once a beautiful hazel, full of life and happiness, his eyes suddenly looked heavy and full of horrors from the past twenty four hours he had just endured.

"I am a monster" he shouted, voice low and gruff – once more he sounded more Wolf than human. I began to really get scared then. "All I can think about is food, but there is nothing to satisfy my needs. All I can think about it sex, but there is nothing to satisfy my needs. All I can think about is murder, but there is nothing to satisfy my needs". He was almost screaming, and I heard Landon take the stairs two at a time in my aid.

"We can get you through this Gavin" I told him, just as the door flew open and Landon stumbled in – ready for a fight. With his raised fists, and wide stance, Gavin instantly saw him as a threat to his survival. He went into primal mode.

Diving at Landon, before either of us could prepare ourselves for an attack, they both went down. Gavin's teeth went for the kill zone; the primal instinct was to kill from the exposed neck. Gavin did that, his teeth trying to rip out Landon's jugular.

But I jumped into action before he had a chance. I shot over to them, grabbing Gavin by the scruff of the neck and throwing him across the room. Like a catapult, he flung threw the air, before crashing into the wall by the bathroom. The wall dented, as he hit it before tumbling to the floor.

Landon scrambled to his feet, but it wasn't quick enough. Even I was shocked by Gavin's speed. The Forced Turn jumped to his feet and charged at me. Before, only Landon was a threat, but I had gone on the attack not the defence, therefore I was also a threat that had to be eliminated.

My leg swung up to deliver a swift kick to Gavin, just before he reached me. He groaned, as my shin slammed into his stomach and winded him. He stumbled back a few steps. I rushed him, ploughing him to the floor before straddling him.

"Landon grab the duct tape from the basement" I hissed. Before I was even finished talking, Landon was sprinting out the door – obeying my command without a momentarily thought. Sometimes, in that instant, the primal instincts were handy. But in other instants, such as Gavin seeing the unknown as a threat, they were also a massive hindrance.

It took Gavin about ten seconds to recover from being winded, before he began to thrash in my arms. The sense of déjà vu sunk in, but the second scuffle was with enhanced strength and speed. I struggled to hold him.

My fingers gripped his wrists, trying to force them to the ground, my nails accidently slicing his skin as I did so. Small droplets of blood ran out. Gavin growled at me, a horrible screech of anger from the back of his throat.

One second I was pinning him, the next he brought his knee up and slammed it into my stomach. I yelled in pain, my grip loosening enough for him to flip me over so that he was pinning me. His teeth shone, as he bared them with a snarl of triumph. I sunk my head into my neck, so that as little of my nape was exposed as possible.

Gavin didn't like me hiding my weak point. He slammed his elbow into my face, instantly breaking my nose. I screamed bloody murder, as stars danced in my vision. I could feel – and smell – the blood over my face. His elbow slammed into my chest next, and I convulsed in pain as I tried to breath without it hurting. Multiple ribs broke.

He raised his elbow once more, aiming for my face again. However, before he had time to slam it down, Landon was back. With the boot of his shoe he slammed into Gavin's side. The pair toppled over me and into the entrance of the bathroom, leaving me dizzy and winded on the bedroom floor.

Landon and Gavin were probably both well matched in strength and speed. However, Landon was untrained and sporadic, and Gavin was a very well trained police officer. The Omega of the Pack didn't stand a chance.

Gavin flipped Landon onto his back, before grabbing a handful of his hair and slamming his face into the floor. Landon screamed in pain, as his head smashed against the tiled floor of the bathroom. Blood pooled around him; scarlet and thick. Landon was out cold within seconds of the blow.

Gavin readied himself for the kill, but I refused to let that happen. If I took his attention away from the hunt, he would no longer see Landon as a threat and therefore not return for the kill. I growled at Gavin – as best as I could with my broken ribs screaming at me just to lie silently until help came. But I was no damsel in fucking distress, and I would not allow my Pack brother to die.

Gavin's head swung around at the sound my feeble growl. Thoughts of Landon gone, he got to his feet and stalked his way over to me. I pushed myself up to my feet, grabbing the bed post to steady me. Every breath was a struggle.

Gavin dived at me, and I went down. Our bodies crashed together, and I choked on a sob of pain, as my head bounced off the bed post. Fresh blood poured from my body, and soaked the carpet as I landed.

I looked up at Gavin, his hazel eyes shining brighter than humanly possible, and I snarled in anger. He returned the sound, as his jaw opened for the kill. But, before he had the chance the sound of a car door made his pause. Saxon and Ernie were back.

Gavin sniffed the air, realising he was largely outnumbered, and growled furiously. My vision danced, as I fought off unconsciousness. Gavin jumped off me, and raced in the direction of the back window. I tried to shout out, so that Saxon would know that Gavin was escaping around the back of the house when he was at the front.

But I couldn't. My ribs hurt, my nose hurt, but worst of all my head hurt. I vaguely heard Saxon call out for me, as he opened the front door, before the world swirled into blackness.

Chapter Twenty One

"Chelsea". My head was thumping, and I could feel bile turning in my stomach. "Come on, Chelsea". Pain was shooting throughout my entire body, and I whimpered. "Chelsea, open your eyes, I'm right here".

I tried to follow the instructions given to me, but I was in so much pain. I pushed through the agony, and my eyes began to flick open – light blinding me. Hands touched my body, and I felt my clothing being removed.

I freaked out. "Chelsea, calm down. It's me, Saxon" a familiar voice whispered into my ear. At the mention of Saxon's name, I relaxed. But I could still hardly see – my vision was blurry and I could just about see the silhouette of the man I was in love with.

"Saxon" I said, choking on a sob. "Saxon, I really hurt".

"I know, Chelsea. I'm right here, I'm right here" he replied. My stomach turned because I could hear the fear and worry in his voice. I whimpered, sobs making me cry. However, with each breath my chest felt like it was about to cave in.

"Saxon get out the way" Ernie growled, but I was too foggy to actually work out where he was. Saxon moved away from me, and I whimpered in sadness that he was gone when I needed him the most. A second later Ernie's blurry shape filled my eyes.

"Where's Saxon?" I whimpered, bottom lip quivering.

"He's right here, Chelsea. But I need you to listen to me" Ernie snapped, a fierceness to his voice. "You need to Shift. You've damaged part of your skull, and if you don't Shift you're going to bleed to death".

"I can't" I sobbed. "Saxon?"

"Dammit Chelsea listen to me. You need to Shift and heal yourself" he growled at me. "Chelsea, fucking pay attention. I know you are in pain, but you need to Shift. Alright?" Even in my hazing, painful, state I could hear the urgency in his voice.

"How?" I groaned out, trying to work everything out slowly.

"Picture yourself as a Wolf. Dark fur, blue eyes, long legs...everything you can remember" Ernie said slowly. I closed my eyes, doing as he said. I felt my clothing being moved, and I whined in pain as it was done.

But slowly, and enormously painfully, my Shift began. Each bone in my body broke, and reformed, and I screamed and screamed and screamed. It was worse than all the other

Shifts I had experienced. I blacked out half way through, and woke up to Ernie encouraging me through the rest of the Shift.

As soon as I was in Wolf form, I lay on my side as I breathed deeply. I must have fallen asleep, due to exhaustion, and when I woke up my body began to Shift back. The second time wasn't as bad as after I was injured, but it still hurt more than normal.

"Hey, Chelsea" Ernie smiled, when I Shifted back. He sat on the bedroom floor, next to where I lay naked on the rug. It was getting dark, so I knew I must have been out of it for most of the day. Ernie moved so he was squatting in front of me. "How you feeling?"

"Like shit" I whispered, voice hoarse. "How long was I out of it?"

"We found you about five hours ago, but after your first Shift you slept for about three hours. You were hazy for the rest of it. You took a bad hit to the head, you're lucky we found you before you bled to death. You'll be sore for a few days, because you lost so much blood".

"How is Landon?"

"Asleep next door, but a lot better than you. Gavin is long gone. I sent Saxon after him, but we lost the trail when he got into a cab. But we'll worry about that later. First, let's just get you better".

"I'm hungry" I mumbled, "and tired". I ran my tongue over my dried lips, and tried to sit up. Ernie helped me up, before walking me over to the bed. Every step was agony, but I couldn't work out where the pain was actually coming from.

Just as Ernie helped me under the bed covers, a knock on the door sounded. A second later, Saxon's head slipped through the door. When he saw me awake, he grinned a bright smile. I returned the smile, but mine was plagued with fatigue.

"I come bearing gifts" he said, walking in with two plates of food. My stomach growled as I took in the scent of the tomato sauce on the pasta. It was basic food, but I was too hungry to care.

"I'll leave you two alone" Ernie smiled, before slipping past Saxon and out the room. He shut the door on us. Saxon's large brown eyes stared at me for a heavy second – relief and joy in his eyes.

"Mind if I join?" he asked, after a second, before nodding to the bed.

"I'd mind if you didn't" I replied, before cuddling further into the pillow. Saxon grinned before climbing into the bed next to me. I snuggled into him, as he carefully placed the plates down. "I'm so hungry" I groaned, as my head rested on top of his chest.

"Here" Saxon grinned, putting some pasta on the fork and bringing it to my mouth. I happily ate the food offered. Saxon chuckled, as he continued to feed me. "I'm sorry I wasn't here. Ernie sent me out. He told me that I was too emotional, and I would just scare you more".

I finished my mouthful, before smiling up at him. "I know you would have been there is you could".

"When I came in and I saw all that blood…" he trailed off, and a shiver went through his body. "What happened?"

"Gavin just freaked out. He started shouting that he was a monster, and all he wanted to do was eat, and fuck, and kill. Landon came running up, worried for me. But, he came in with his fists raised. He was ready for a fight".

"And Gavin saw him as a threat, and attacked".

"Yeah" I nodded, before taking the next mouthful that Saxon offered me. "We have to go after him, don't we?" I asked, after I swallowed. I took the next forkful, as he answered.

"He's dangerous. We have to go after him before he completely loses control. At the moment, he think he is a monster. But if given the time, he'll actually turn into one".

"We should get going now" I stated, sitting up in the bed. I cringed in pain as I did so.

"No, we need to get you and Landon healthy again. Then, we'll go after him". He pressed a kiss to the side of my head, before raising the fork to my lips. I took another bite.

"How does my nose look?" I asked, remembering the way Gavin had smashed the bone with his elbow.

"Perfect" Saxon replied, playfully pressing a kiss to the tip of it. I chuckled and swatted him away. He laughed as well, before raising his hand to feed me once more.

"I feel a lot better now. Let me feed myself now" I said, taking the fork from him. Saxon frowned, but didn't argue. I ate in silence for a while, before Saxon relaxed and put his arm around me. Once I finished the food, I was still hungry, but not enough to complain.

"You should get some sleep. We'll set after Gavin in the morning" Saxon said, pressing another kiss to the side of my head.

"Will you stay with me?" I smiled, sliding down into the bed and Saxon followed me.

"Of course I will. I couldn't sleep without you last night" he replied, as I cuddled into his embrace. His words sent warm shivers through my body. I loved that he needed me as much as I needed him. He flicked the lights off, and we cuddled up together.

We were silent for a while, before I opened my eyes to see Saxon watching me closely. "You can't sleep if you have your eyes open" I commented with a small smirk. Saxon chuckled, his hot breath blowing over me.

"I might not be able to fall asleep, but I can fall in love" he replied, and my smile was gone in a second. His gold speckled eyes glistened as they stared into mine. I gulped, pretty sure my heart was about to pound out of my chest. "Chelsea" Saxon whispered, voice heavy. It was all I needed, that one word full of need and want.

My lips crashed into his, my arms throwing themselves around Saxon's neck. His lips were everything I dreamed they were. I drank them in greedily; they were soft yet firm, but with a sweet hint to them. The simple kiss had my heart beating at dangerous speeds.

My skin brushed against his stubble, as our lips battled passionately. Saxon's tongue teased my lips, as I pressed my body closer to his. My lungs burnt in pain, but I didn't even care because I was so in love. But I had to breathe. I pulled away, cringing in pain.

"Sorry, sorry. I forgot" Saxon gushed, pushing my hair out of my face as he moved the covers away so that I had more room to breathe. "Are you alright?" he worried, as I pushed myself into a sitting position.

"I'm better than I've ever been" I grinned at him. "I've wanted to do that for so long".

Saxon chuckled, "me too. Since the moment I met you". Leaning forward, his lips briefly brushed mine. He pulled away when the door opened. Landon walked in, a goofy smile on his lips. He paused when he saw how close Saxon and I were.

"Am I interrupting something?" he questioned, lips smirking softly.

"No. Are you alright?" Saxon asked – he was just as worried for his second Turn as he had been for me.

"I can't sleep well. Just keep thinking of Gavin" he shrugged, an almost embarrassed look crossing his face. I shared a look with Saxon, and he gave a small nod in understanding. We put our Pack before ourselves.

"We're going to bed, come join us" I smiled, opening the covers. Landon walked over and slipped in beside me. I cuddled into his chest, as Saxon pressed into my back.

"I love you guys" Landon said, through a large yawn.

"We love you too" I laughed, as my eyes began to drop. Saxon pressed a soft kiss to my neck, which made the remaining tension in my shoulders disappear. I fell asleep firmly pressed between the two men I cared about most in the world.

Chapter Twenty Two

Ernie had followed Gavin's scent north, to where he had stolen a car and driven south. The following morning, when he returned, Saxon showed us why he was such a good a private investigator. Firing up his laptop, he managed to find everything we needed to find about Officer Gavin Lorraine.

After that he hacked into the police database, and found the car that had been stolen – from where Ernie confirmed the scent for Gavin weeded out. "Alright, so we have the car he's driving. How's that going to help us?" Landon questioned.

"Because I am currently waiting to find out which direction he is heading, so that we can follow him".

"How do you do that?" I questioned, finding it amazing how good Saxon was on a computer. I mean I could do the basic of things on a computer, but watching him work made my head hurt.

"The car is registered stolen, so every time he goes past a police camera, his plates will flash up. I'm just waiting for the results of that to work out which direction he is heading" Saxon answered.

"Wow, you're really clever" I commented, and he offered me a bright smile. I wanted so badly to kiss him again, but decided against it. We'd shared amazing, heart racing, kisses that I never wanted to stop experiences.

But we had woken up that morning, and I looked at Saxon and he smiled and pressed a kiss to my cheek – my fucking cheek! I thought we were past the cheek kissing, but obviously we had taken one step forward and ten steps back with our relationship. However, I was so in love with him that even just knowing he felt *something* for me, was enough to make me feel like I had won the lottery.

"You know I can't come with you kids, right?" Ernie said, pulling my thoughts away from Saxon for a few minutes.

"Why not?" I demanded, frowning.

"I have a big lecture on Monday morning, not to mention Allie will be coming home tomorrow. I have a life that doesn't involve following Forced Turns across the goddamn country to stop him becoming a man-eater" he told me.

"A man-eater? Is that common?" Landon asked, taking the question straight from my mouth.

"Not with normal Turns, but with Force Turns, yes. They are more primal and--"

"And they have a hunger that can't be satisfied" I finished dryly. I frowned deeply, remembering what Gavin had told me the night before. I couldn't help but feel disgusted by the thought of a man-eater, especially since I would feel guilty as I could have possible stopped Gavin from escaping and killing people.

As if sensing my thoughts, Saxon placed his hand on my thigh and gave it a squeeze. I offered him a small smile, as he kept his hand there and it warmed my insides "We'll get him, Chels" he promised.

"We can't ask Ernie to come anyway" Saxon sighed heavily – the stress evident in his eyes. "I created this mess, I have to deal with it".

I pecked his cheek, "no, *we* have to deal with it". My words made Landon nod; we would both do whatever it took to help our Sire. Gavin was dangerous, but it was our job to stop him before he got anyone else hurt, or worse killed.

Landon and I packed up our things, and I packed up Saxon's, before loading them into the car. Saxon stayed at his computer, fingers tapping crazily as he familiarised himself with exactly who Gavin was.

"Guys" Saxon exclaimed – Landon and I were in front of him in a second. "Gavin spends his summers is New Orleans. He went to college up there after high school, but dropped out after his mother got sick and moved back. However, every summer he goes back to New Orleans to party all summer with the friends he has out there".

"How did you find all that out?" I asked in disbelief.

"You'll never believe what you can find out from Facebook and other social media sites".

"So he likes to fuck girls and wear beads. How does that help us in anyway?" Landon snorted.

"Because ten minutes ago the car he stole flashed up a camera for speeding. Just on the border of Louisiana".

"So you think he's going to stay with the friends he has in New Orleans" I breathed out, in understanding. Saxon confirmed with a nod, as he quickly closed his laptop down. "I'll drive" I said, grabbing the car keys as Landon helped Saxon put his PI equipment away.

In the kitchen, I ran past Ernie, pressing a kiss on his cheek as I shouted goodbye – before sprinting out the door. Landon called shotgun and dived in next to me, as Saxon practically fell into the back in his haste. I hit the gas the moment the doors closed.

"Ease up, we don't want to get stopped on the way" Landon complained, as I roared down Ernie's driveway. I slowed down slightly, but was still well over the speed limit.

Five hours into the drive, we stopped at a drive thru, and got enough food to make the server's eyebrows shoot up. Landon then took over the driving, as I ate as much as I could manage. Saxon was still worried about my injuries – even though my Shift had healed them, I was still in slight pain. I assured him I was fine, but he encouraged me to have his share of the food. I didn't argue; I was starving.

When night came, and both Landon and Saxon had done a few hours of driving, we swapped once more. I took over again, as Saxon slipped into the passenger's side; neither of us wanting to wake Landon, who had been snoring from the back since he's finished his driving shift.

Saxon fired up his laptop, as I pulled away from the sidewalk. "You should get some sleep" I said, as his fingers tapped at a ridiculously fast pace.

"We should be in New Orleans within the next five hours. I can last until then".

"But when we get there, you're going to instantly want to find Gavin" I replied.

"You haven't slept either".

"I don't feel tired".

"Well neither do I" he retorted, and I sighed. "Chels, if anyone needs rest, it's you. You had your skull beaten in last night, and most of your ribs broken. Yet you're worried about me". He shook his head, giving a small humourless laugh.

"I'm more worried about your mental state" I admitted honestly.

"You think I'm slowly going crazy? Because that was what Ernie thinks too".

"Not like that. I just worry that all of this; all the death, all the bodies and now with Gavin...I just worry you won't ever go back to that happy-go-lucky man you were when I met you" I told him. Saxon was silent for a moment, biting down on his bottom lip as he thought.

"You keep bringing me back" he said after a while.

"What?"

"I keep losing myself, keep hating myself a little more each time I kill someone. But then, there you are. Beautiful, and radiant, and pure. And I remember that even if I do nothing else good in my life, I will know that at least I Turned you. I helped bring you into the Pack's life, and I know that you will be the best thing to ever happen to them too".

"Saxon--"

"No, let me finish. I have to say this now, or I might never get the courage again. When I'm with you I feel like there is a purpose to all this. You are like a new dawn on a dark day, you come and remind me that there is still good in the world. I told you I don't really have anyone I'm close to, but I want to be close to you. I want to always be close to you".

I was silent for a while, before I slowed the car and pulled over. "Why are you stopping?" Saxon asked, confused. I turned off the car engine and turned to face him. In the dark, the gold in his eyes seem to shine and his broad figure made him look larger.

"Because if I kiss you when I'm driving I might crash" I said, before leaning over and taking his face in my hands. I pressed my lips to his, and he quickly returned the kiss with intense need. And I understood – I needed him too, I needed him so much.

"Now I'm *really* not tired" Saxon joked, when we pulled away. I couldn't help but breath out a laugh, as I rested my forehead against his. "We shouldn't be doing this" he whispered, but there was a wicked smile on his face. "We have to find Gavin, after that we can spend all day doing this, and so much more". He pecked my lips. "But for now, we have to keep going".

Chapter Twenty Three

Saxon and I sent Landon to book us a motel, and get us dinner, as soon as we arrived in New Orleans. Saxon and I then caught a cab to the French Quarter. "I guess it's true what they say, every night in New Orleans *really* is party night" Saxon muttered, shocked.

"You're telling me you've never been to New Orleans for Mardi Gras?" I laughed, as we weaved through the streets full of people – they were all drunk as it was just before three in the morning. And, well, it was New Orleans.

Saxon shot me a glance, "do I look like the type of person who does keg stands and has one night stands?"

I laughed, "you're missing out. Maybe I'll bring you next year".

"As much as I'd love to go on holiday with you. I'm not much of a drinker, so I don't know how much fun I would be". A soft blush filled his cheeks as I laughed. After the first time Saxon had lost a person to his bite, we had shared our woes over a bottle of tequila. I had the majority of the bottle, whereas he only had a few drinks and passed out before I did. I knew from that moment that Saxon was not a drinker.

"So when you were you in high school?" I asked, as we maneuverer around a group of giggling girls.

"What about it?"

"Look at you, Sax, you're seriously hot. Surely, you were super popular and were invited to parties every night". I smiled up at Saxon, but quickly realised that he wasn't smiling back. Saxon was silent for a moment. "Sorry, we should be focusing on Gavin. How much longer until we reach his friend's bar?"

He glanced at the phone in his hand, "it's just around the corner. Five minutes maybe". Taking my hand in his, he led me through the streets of the French Quarter. His hand in mine was a small comfort in the tension filled night.

A group of drunk twenty-somethings crashed into us, giggling and laughing. They slipped some beads over our heads, laughing manically as Saxon awkwardly thanked them. We left the pink beads around our neck, as we carried on weaving through the crowds of dancing people.

"When this is all over will you let me show you the good parts of New Orleans?" I questioned, as we reached the street.

"I told you I don't drink".

"You don't have to drink to have a good time, Saxon. I'll make sure you have the best night ever when all this is over". I gave his hand a squeeze, as he smiled tightly at me. We reached the busy bar, which Gavin's friend owned, and slipped inside.

"Plan?" I asked, as we headed towards the bar.

"I'll questioned Mr Sanders about whether he's seen Gavin, and you scout the area" Saxon whispered back. I nodded, before letting go of his hand. He carried on his way to the bar, to ask for the owner, as I moved into the thick of the dancefloor.

Trying to look casual, I swayed with the music as I zigged and zagged through the parting people. A few men tried to dance with me, but I carried on pushing past them. I tried to pick up Gavin's scent, but there were too many people around for me to decipher anything.

I needed to get closer to the ground if I wanted to try and filter the different scents. Digging into my pocket, I pulled the loose change from it. Getting to the edge of the dancefloor, I dropped the dimes to the floor.

I got to my knees, and began to scoop up my dropped change. As I did so, I leant as close to the ground as possible and took a deep inhale. My nose could smell everything; alcohol, drugs, sweat, sex – I could smell it all. It was easier for me to filter the scents I was already familiar with, as my nostrils wanted to explore all the new scents.

But I focused my mind, and filtered all the different scents as I searched for Gavin's. And, then, I found it. Gavin's musky, earthy, scent made my senses go wild. My instincts went wild – I had found the threat, so I wanted to follow it.

I had found a Pack mate, so I wanted to be happy. I had found the scent Saxon wanted, so I wanted to please my Sire and tell him.

Standing up I fought against the other instincts, and went after Gavin. I tracked him through the dancefloor, noticing that his scent mingled with another. He had found himself a date. That scared me; but both scents were fresh, so I knew they couldn't have been gone too long.

I glanced at the bar, with no sign of Saxon. I assumed he had taken Gavin's friend into a back room for privacy. I wanted to go to him, but I also knew I couldn't let Gavin go away. So I pushed against the mental argument, and I went after Gavin. I had allowed him to get away from me once, I had to prove that it wouldn't happen again.

The scent led me out of the bar, and into the busy street. A jazz band was playing loudly – their fast melody filling the streets and allowing the beat to cause movement in people's bodies. Dancing people, both drunk and sober, lined the streets shouting and singing.

I knew it was too much to want a quiet night in New Orleans; but that was all I could wish for in that very moment. Because everyone was dancing around me, and bumping into me. I was trying so hard to focus on Gavin's scent, but with so many other smells around it was so hard.

As I exited the French Quarter, I lost the scent and had to retrace my steps. Once I found it again, I quickly picked up my pace. The other scent was still intertwined with Gavin's. He was taking a woman home for the night, and the longer I took the less likely it was that the women would remain unharmed.

Gavin was once a nice guy – well, I assumed he was a nice guy. I did not know Gavin before the Turn so I couldn't really comment on that. But the man I saw before the fever hit was someone I imagined I would have liked, and even have become good friends with. But after the Forced Turn, that man was dead.

Gavin was unpredictable. And that – matched with enhanced strength and speed – made the ultimate dangerous combination. Gavin was dangerous, and the quicker we stopped him the better.

I left the busy night life of New Orleans behind me, where I found myself in a housing project. The streets were dark, lit softly by flickering street lamps, which cast long shadows of the empty streams. The low heels on my boots clicked on the sidewalk, echoing in the early morning darkness.

I followed Gavin's scent to a large apartment block. At the door, I ran my hand over all the buzzers – knowing that at least one person would buzz me in. A second later, the door clicked open and I walked inside.

I walked slowly up the stairs, with my hood up as I worried there was security cameras, and I wasn't sure how everything was going to pan out. I struggled following Gavin's scent, when I reached the second floor. There was too many fresh scents, of other people who lived there.

I bent down on the top of the stairwell, and tried to sort through the scents. But my sense of smell wasn't as good as my hearing, and I failed. Cussing softly under my breath, I stood back up and pushed the doors for the second floor. I walked past all the door, both listening and sniffing. Nothing. So I went up a level, and again, nothing.

Finally, on the top level, I picked up scent which had my feet breaking in a run. It wasn't just Gavin's scent, it was Gavin's scent intertwined with blood. I was too late. I realised that, in the moment I ran down the corridor of the fourth floor.

When I reached the apartment door, where the scent of blood was coming from, I reached for the handle. Then, I froze. I couldn't guarantee what was inside, so I didn't want to spread my fingertips everywhere.

Taking a step back, I kicked the door in with my boot. The wooden door splintered down the middle, and caved in on itself. I used my clothed arm to push the wood to the floor, and step inside. A wave of blood and death hit me, and I gagged.

I moved inside the apartment cautiously, over stepping the mess of empty alcohol bottles and dirty clothing. I listened as I moved, not picking up any heartbeats in the room – I could hear the people in the room next door, but not in the apartment. No one was alive in the apartment, I was sure of that.

The strongest scent of blood was coming from the bedroom, I made my way over. The door was pulled closed, and a large part of me really didn't want to open the door. But I didn't have a choice.

Using my boot again, I nudged the door open. It flew open, quicker than I wanted, and the scent of blood and sex hit me. I gagged, as I clamped my eyes shut. I really, really, really, didn't want to open my eyes. But I had to. I had to see what Gavin had done.

I held my breath, as my lids slowly opened. My heart sped up, and my stomach turned, with what I saw. A tall, brown haired, woman lay naked on her own bed. Her wrists, and ankles were bound to the bed posts with fabric. She had been stabbed multiple times, and parts of her stomach and lower intestines were over the bed. I could see that parts of her had been eaten.

Then, just when I thought it couldn't get any worse, I heard sirens in the distance. And they were coming my way.

Chapter Twenty Four

I phoned Saxon when I got a block away from the motel. "Chels, where the hell did you go?" Saxon said immediately. I was running, so my breathing was heavy on the receiver. I had climbed out the window of the apartment block, dropped down onto balconies, before reaching the bottom and running off into the night. I watched the cops turn up five minutes later, and I heard them find the woman's body. After that, I ran as fast I could.

"Get back to the motel. Now" I hissed, not saying any more before hanging up. Encase someone had seen me at the apartments, I didn't need them checking my messages if I became a suspect in a homicide. So I would have to tell Saxon and Landon everything in person.

Landon was watching something questionable when I flew through the door. He instantly changed the channel. "The TV turned onto that channel, I swear" he rambled nervously, a blush highlighting his dark skin.

"I don't care, just turn it off".

"What happened?" Landon asked, switching the TV off, before walking over to me. He could see that I was not only spooked, but also worried. He knew that something was wrong.

"Shit didn't just hit the fan, it hit the fucking propeller" I breathed out. Landon didn't ask anymore, he just took me in his arms. And in that moment, it was the only thing I needed. I curled into his embrace, head resting against his, as his arms held me with strength.

A few seconds later, Saxon blew through the door. I instantly moved away from Landon, and through myself at the man I loved. "Chels" he cooed, as I pressed my face into his chest and wrapped my arms around his waist. He didn't ask me anything, just ran his hands through my hair and pressed a gentle kiss to my head.

I pulled back after a few minutes, and looked up into Saxon's dark eyes and all I wanted to do was kiss him. He offered me a sad smile, obviously wanting the same, before he simply tucked my hair behind my ear and moved away from me.

"Landon get her some water" Saxon said, and his youngest Sire obeyed instantly. Saxon pulled me over to the bed, and sat me on the edge of it. He pulled up a chair in front of me, and took a seat. His large, soft, palm rested on my knee. Landon came back with a mug of water, and I instantly gulped it down.

"Now, take a deep breath and tell us what happened".

"He's a man-eater" I whispered, my voice low and gentle – but they both still heard. Saxon sucked a deep breath in, and Landon muttered something colourful under his breath. With shaking hands I pulled my phone from my hands. I handed the phone to Saxon. "I took pictures".

Saxon unlocked my phone, and looked through the two quick snaps I had managed to get before running. Landon gagged when he saw the pictures, and turned away in disgust. Saxon had his business face on, and simply frowned.

"What happened?" Saxon asked, pocketing my phone. I looked into his eyes; which were soft but full of strength. I drew my own strength from them, and told him everything that happened.

"You shouldn't have gone without me" he sighed, when I finished my story.

"I handled it, didn't I?" I snapped, not liking the implication that I was weak.

Saxon looked offended, "of course you did. I would never doubt you could handle anything, I just mean that you shouldn't have had to go through that by yourself. I know you can do it, you just shouldn't have to".

"Sorry" I muttered, feeling warmed by his words.

"Chelsea, you go and get a shower. The food is cold now anyway, so we might as well eat it after. I'll try and see if I can pick anything up on the police's database. Landon you ring Ernie and let him know what happened with Gavin" Saxon told us, and we both instantly obliged.

The warm water of the shower didn't help wash away the memories – and those were the one thing that I wanted to be washed into the drain. Once I stepped out of the shower, and dried myself with a towel, I headed back into the room.

Landon was in the bed, yawning largely. If he hadn't have only just Turned, I would be annoyed because he slept most of the drive. But I slept for about three days after my Turn, so I understood. I offered him a small smile, as I turned to Saxon.

My Sire sat in the corner of the room, in a tattered arm chair, with his computer on his lap. "Sax, you alright?" I asked. He glanced up at me; eyes poking out from above his laptop.

"Just trying to see if I can either hack into the police database, or see if there has been any activity on Gavin's credit card. Maybe then we can see where he was saying" he replied, offering me a sad smile. His words reminded me of Gavin's friends.

"What did the bar owner say?" I asked.

"Not much. Gavin had come in to have a drink with him. He said Gavin was acting weird, and he called him out on it. Apparently Gavin freaked out, and left. He hadn't seen him since. Made no mention of him staying the night, or any ideas of his plans".

"So a dead end?"

"Not necessarily. Gavin's world is falling apart, and he's going to try and grasp as much of his old life as he can. So, I'm actually banking on the fact that he's going to go back to his friend's house" Saxon told me. "Plus, I think he was lying – his heart beat was irregular".

"Do you want me to go over and watch his house?" I asked, eager.

"No" Saxon stated instantly. "You're been through enough tonight. You two get some sleep. I'll wake Landon up after a few hours, and he can go over". From the bed, Landon nodded in understanding.

"I don't mind--"

"But I do" Saxon cut my arguments off. I frowned, and he smiled softly at me again. "You're still recovering, and then you went through this. Please, just eat some pizza, and get some sleep. We'll regroup in the morning".

I couldn't argue with that. So we ate two cold pizzas between us, before Saxon carried on with his investigating, while Landon and I went to bed. I cuddled up with my Pack brother, and allowed myself to drift off into a well needed sleep.

I woke up, when I heard Landon leaving to watch over Gavin's friends. The shutting of the motel door, shocked me out of my slumber, and I sat up in the bed. I blinked away the sleep, as my eyes focused on the room. Saxon still sat in the armchair, laptop on his lap.

Silently slipping out of the bed, the cold air blew over my nude body. I walked over to Saxon, but he was too focused on his computer to notice. I reached out, and plucked the laptop from his grip. He jumped, before he looked up at me. "You need to sleep" I told him, closing the computer and placing it on the side.

"We need to find Gavin" he argued. "I'll sleep afterwards".

"No you won't. You're the most experienced tracker we have, and we don't need you making mistakes because you haven't slept. Landon is out there, and he will phone us if there is anything wrong". I took his hand and pulled him up from the chair.

I walked over to the bed, and pulled Saxon along with me. I took a seat on the edge of the bed, as he removed his clothing. I had seen Saxon naked practically every day since I had met him; but right then, I actually took notice.

His large, muscled, chest seemed to glimmer in the dark motel room – his skin pale and clear. My eyes trailed over his six pack, before my eyes travelled downwards. There were strong indentation of his skin, in a thick V formation, leading down his hip bones. I followed them greedily with my eyes, before I found my eyes focusing in on his intimidate area.

I knew I shouldn't have been looking at it, but I couldn't help it. His member was pronounced, and large, with a thick vein running through it. I swallowed deeply; not being able to not be turned on in that moment.

"Chelsea" Saxon whispered, his voice hoarse and thick. My eyes snapped away, and looked up to his face. His dark eyes were staring at me, his jaw sharp from biting down. "I can smell your arousal".

I never had a problem with sex before. I had never been short of male attention, and I had never been scared of it. I was confident, and adventurous, and was never afraid of showing emotions. Yet, I blushed the moment Saxon told me he could smell my sexual arousal. I loved him so much that I desperately wanted to act 'correctly' but I didn't know what that was.

"I'm sorry" I whispered, looking down. Saxon knelt in front of me, before he gripped my chin and forced my eyes back up.

"Don't be. I want you so much".

Butterflies fluttered around my stomach, "I'm nervous".

"You don't strike me as the shy type" Saxon smirked, a deep chuckling rumbling his chest.

"Usually I'm not. But this is different. This is us" I admitted. Saxon and I looked into each other's eyes for a long moment, but I made the first move. Leaning forward, I pressed my lips to his. The kiss was gentle, and soft to begin with. But the longer the kiss went on, the hungrier and more forceful the kiss began.

As soon I smelt his arousal, and felt his heat, my confidence came shooting back. He wanted me, just as much as I wanted him. Throwing my arms around his neck, I pulled him closer and Saxon's hands grabbed my wide hips.

I moved back onto the bed, and pulled Saxon with me. Not breaking the kiss, he followed me and hovered over me. I wrapped my legs around his waist, and pulled his hips down so they pressed into mine. As soon as I felt his erection poke into me, a shiver went through my spine.

My fingers dug into back, as my tips brushed over the muscles in his back. Saxon pulled his lips away from mine, and feathered kisses down to my neck. My eyes slid shut in blissfulness, as his hands ran up my sides before cupping my chest.

His callous hands struggled to cover my large breasts, but Saxon gave it a good go – his hands squeezing the skin as his teeth nipped at my neck. Another shiver ranked my spine, and I arched into Saxon's hands.

I felt a wetness on my upper thigh, that wasn't my own, and realised that pre-excitement was already leaking out of Saxon's hard erection. Just thinking about how turned on he was, had a moan leaked through lips.

Hearing my eagerness, Saxon's lips returned to mine, and his hands gripped onto my hips once more. He raised himself up, before positioning himself at my entrance. "You sure?" he asked, laboured breathing turning me on even more.

"Never been more sure of anything in my life" I replied, and he smiled brightly. He pressed another kiss to my lips, before he raised my hips slightly and slid into me. I moaned loudly as he did so. He fit me snuggly. "Oh, Chelsea" Saxon moaned, his voice full of arousal and content.

As he pulled out, I glanced up into his beautiful eyes. It was then my turn to moan his name, as he thrusted roughly into me. Saxon picked up a fast pace; pumping in and out of me, as his hands gripped my sides. We rocked back and forward, the motel bed creaking loudly as we kept pace. We went on for a long while – both of us having Werewolf stamina to keep going.

I felt myself climaxing, and my head flopped back slightly. I moaned loudly, almost a scream, as my entire body shook. Saxon continued to push in and out of me; quick and deep. It didn't take me long to reach my high, and my abdomen muscles contracted tightly. My breath hitched and I was so overwhelmed that I couldn't make a sound.

After Saxon finished himself, he pulled out of me, and we lay next to each other – both of us breathing heavily, and our chests heaving. I looked into his eyes, and my heart thumped harder. I loved him so much, but I was too scared to tell him. So I simply cuddled as close to Saxon as I could, and fell asleep completely satisfied.

Chapter Twenty Five

Landon found no sign of Gavin, so when we met him for breakfast – in a large colourful diner – we had to devise a new plan. Landon, Saxon and I ate as much as we could, as Saxon did a bit more research on Gavin Lorraine.

"Hey guys" Landon hissed, cutting off a conversation Saxon and I were having. We both turned to look where he was pointing across the diner. A small wall mounted TV was showing the news highlights. "She kind of looks you" he muttered, as they showed a picture of Gavin's kill – she was pretty when she wasn't half eaten

"Hey, can you turn that up?" I asked one of the waitresses. She quickly turned the volume up. The story of the murder had broken already. But it didn't mention the cannibalism aspect or any details really – just that the girl was called

Lauren Powers, and she had been raped and murdered in her own apartment.

"The police department is the first place to start, surely?" I asked, when the news moved on. "We need to make sure there was no leads back to Gavin from last night. Because I don't know about you guys, but I think our priority needs to be to find him before the police find him".

"Exactly" Saxon nodded, his hand secretly resting on my thigh under the table. His hand felt almost naughty, but exciting. I pretended it wasn't there, because we were working, but I could feel the warmth of his hand and it warmed my soul.

"But how do we get close enough to listen?" Landon asked.

"Let me worry about that" I said, "only one of us will need to go the police station. Saxon you should stay seeing what you can find out about Gavin's friends, and what he usually does when he visits. Landon I want you to go to the apartment building, and see if you can pick up a trail for Gavin. I tried last night, but with the sirens coming, I was in a bit of a rush". Both men nodded at me, and Saxon's hand squeezed my thigh.

We finished eating, and Landon went off towards the apartment, Saxon lingered around a moment. "You're alright?" he frowned, worry creasing his forehead.

"I have you, how can I not be alright?" I teased, getting up on my tiptoe and pressing a kiss to his lips. His frowned deeper.

"Chelsea, I'm serious. What you saw last night was heavy, I just want to make sure you're alright".

"Sax, honestly, I'm fine". I kissed him again, not being able to help myself. He tasted so amazing that I just wanted to keep tasting and tasting and tasting.

"You have any ideas how you're going to get into the police station to hear about the girl?"

"I'll think of something when I get in there. Maybe a little redirection for the search" I shrugged.

"False witness statement? That's risky, Chels, I don't want you getting caught in a lie by the cops".

"And I don't want all of us to have to break Gavin out of jail, do you?" I didn't need an answer, and Saxon knew it. He sighed, before offering me a small smile. He kissed me one last time, before throwing me his car keys and heading back to the motel with his laptop.

I drove to the police station, mentally spinning lies I could use. I couldn't deny that I was nervous about lying to the police, but it was necessary. In my life I had been told to avoid cops – I was a stripper, with dodgy relationships with men and drugs, so the police were something I had learnt to avoid.

I parked the car around the block, and walked the few meters to the police station. I walked inside, and even though it was New Orleans I was shocked with how busy the place was. Hungover people, drunk people, high people, and all manner of people behaving badly. Cops lined all the rooms, chatting and doing paperwork.

I walked up to the desk, and the receptionist looked up at me. "What can I do for you, hon?" she asked.

"I want to talk to the police officer, about that murder last night" I replied – my nervousness helping me out. The women pouted her lips, before telling me to wait a moment. She disappeared and returned a few minutes later.

A tall officer, with spiky black hair and thick eyebrows, followed the receptionist. "Hiya, Miss, my name is Officer McCann, I heard you need to talk to someone".

"Yes, Sir, it's about that girl, Lauren Powers. I saw her last night, and I saw who she left with" I told him, battering my eyes softly.

"Let me just clear a questioning room, and I'll take your statement, Miss…"

"Russel. Chelsea Russel" I told him, with a small smile.

"Right, come with me, Miss Russel" Officer McCann said. Even though he was professional, I could see the way his eyes lingered a little too long on me. He led me to the pit of the offices, and told me to take a seat on an empty waiting chair. He then went and got another cop dealing with the case. I took the chance to listen in to everything around me.

I filtered through a handful of conversations, until I heard something interesting. "I tried to get the security tape at the bar, where the victim's cell phone last had activity, but the owner said that his camera wasn't working last night" one cop said.

"Convenient" another cop replied. I was glad there was no connection to Gavin that far. Not much more was said, so I listen to some other conversations for more information. But there was nothing else of interest. And, a few minutes later the cop returned with his colleague.

"Miss Russel I presume?" the other cop said, smiling softly at me. He was an elder man, with light hair and eyes, but a harsh face. "My name is Detective Muir, and Officer McCann and I will be taking your statement. If you'd like to follow me".

Inside a questioning room, I spouted my best bullshit. I spun a story about how I had been at the Spectacle Bar, and a man – white, blonde hair, blue eyes – had approached me. I have a boyfriend so I turned him down, but then later that night I saw him leave with Lauren Powers. I didn't think anything of it, until I saw the news that morning.

Detective Muir wrote everything down, and asked me questions. "Miss Russel, what time was it that the man approached you?"

"Fairly early, about twelve" I replied.

"And what time did you see him leave with Miss Powers".

"About an hour later. They danced and drank together a while" I lied. Detective Muir opened his mouth to answer another question, but a knock came on the door, and another cop came in before he could answer.

"I got that forensic report" he told him, and my ears pricked up. The two cops apologised to me, and told me they'd just be a moment, before slipping out the room. I strained my hearing.

"What does it say?" Detective Muir asked.

"Death by blood loss from the stab wounds. The organs were removed post mortem, and the sexual assault was both post and pre mortem" the cop reported. I filed all that information away.

"Any luck with prints on the knife yet?" Officer McCann questioned, and my heart thumped a little harder.

"Nothing yet. The lab are still working on it" he replied. "Is that a family member you got in there?"

"No a witness. Thinks the assailant tried it on with her first, before leaving with the victim".

The other cop gave a low whistle, "he's got a type. Not that I blame him, she's a real looker. Thought they were related. I'd never get a girl like that to even look at me, so he must be using his good looks to pull the girls in".

"Looks like it. Hey, let me know what the results of those prints get back".

"Sure, will do, Muir" the cop said, before walking away. Detective Muir and Officer McCann returned, and took the last of my statement. They then took my contact details, and said if they needed any more they would get in contact with me.

As I walked out the station, my phone rang. It was Landon. "Chels, Gavin is here. Get here now" he hissed out, and even before he finished talking I was running to my car. I was not letting Gavin get away, again.

Chapter Twenty Six

Saxon drove a nice car, but after I was done with it, it didn't look 'nice'. I drove with the gas pedal pressed tightly to the ground, as I used the hands free to call Saxon. "Hi" he greeted me, and for a moment I just marvelled at the beautiful tone of his voice. Then, as I skidded around the corner, the seriousness of the situation came screeching back to me just like the wheels on the uneven road.

"Landon just called. Gavin just turned up outside the bar" I exclaimed.

Saxon cussed, "alright I'm on my way now".

"Okay" I breathed out.

"Chels?"

"Yeah?" I swerved manically around another corner, getting cursed out by a group of pedestrians when I almost ran them over.

"Be careful, alright? I don't want him hurting you again" he told me sweetly. "I lo--" he began, and my heart sped up rapidly. "Just don't do anything stupid" he finished off, and my heart slowed down. I felt bitterly disappointed as I knew what I wanted him to say, but also excited because I was pretty sure I knew what he wanted to say.

We said our goodbyes, and I quickly reached the bar where Lauren Powers had been abducted by Gavin. I jumped from the car, and raced inside, my heart pounding in a different way than it did with Saxon. I was both excited and nervous at the same time.

Inside, the bar was quiet for New Orleans but busy for a morning. Soft jazz music filled the air, mixed with light conversation and chatter. I looked around at the mundane scene at that moment; shocked that there was no chaos. But, that was good, that was how we wanted to keep it. Because chaos meant Gavin wasn't on a murderous rampage, and if Gavin wasn't on a murderous rampage, well, that was a fucking miracle in itself.

Straining my hearing, I listened for either Landon or Gavin. I didn't hear either, but I heard shouting. And in my experience shouting was never good. So I headed in that direction, hoping I stumbled across either Gavin or Landon. I wasn't sure which man I wanted to find first.

The shouting was coming from upstairs, in the flat above where the owner of the bar lived. I dived behind the bar, and one of the bartenders shouted at me. I sent him a seductive smile, "I'm friends with Gavin and Drakel. They said I could go straight up".

"Drake said that?" the bartender frowned. Drakel Sanders was Gavin's friend, and the owner of the bar, but I hadn't actually met him as of yet.

"Sure, I stayed over last night and I just went out for breakfast. He said I could just walk back in" I lied, offering him a heated look. His eyes widened when he realised what I had meant, but I could see the impressive look that he had for his friend.

"Alright, you know where you're going, right?" he asked, "I don't need you wondering around".

"I'm good" I smiled, before easing the door open and running up the stairs. The shouting grew louder the closer I got.

"Just move the fuck back" a hoarse male voice screamed.

"Just put the gun down" Landon replied, his voice even but I could hear the edge of fear there. I swore mentally, as I came to a stop outside the door. "Chelsea be careful" Landon shouted to me, as my hand wrapped around the door. Before I could turn the handle, the door was ripped open. I came face to face with Gavin.

He looked different than I remember – his auburn hair wild, his eyes wild, his face wild. He was wild, and there was no taming him anymore. He had raped, and murdered, and eaten people. There was nothing to save anymore, because Gavin Lorraine had gone, all that was left was a shell of the former man. A dangerous, murderous, shell.

"Chelsea" he whispered, voice almost a growl. There was a tone in his voice, a tone I recognised well – because it was the way that Saxon said my name when we had been intimate the night before. It was a tone full of want, and need, and lust. He was desperate for me, and that made me feel physically sick.

Behind Gavin, Landon stood against the back window and another man – Drake I presumed – was pointing a gun at him with shaky hands. "Come in, Chelsea, come in" Gavin whispered, eyes piercing my body and making me feel violated in the worst way.

"Tell your friend to put the gun down, Gavin. No one else needs to get hurt here". I walked slowly into the room, hands up in a surrender and making my neck as long as possible – offering him my most vulnerable part; an easy kill method. I was playing on Gavin's primal instincts to show him I was no threat. It was a lie, I was the biggest threat there.

Gavin shut the door behind me, and I tried to not keep eye contact with me. He wanted to be the dominant, and the aggressor, so I would allow that to him. I had to play into his hand, because until that gun was put away I didn't have a chance against him.

"Go stand over there" Drake growled out, pointing to Landon.

"No, she stays with me" Gavin argued, grabbing my arm and pulling me to him. I crashed into his side, and he growled at the contact. "I told you. I just want her, and then we can get out of here".

Drake's eyes roamed over me. "She does look like that girl last night, hotter though. You say we can have her?"

"You can't have her, she doesn't belong to you" Landon snapped.

"Shut your mouth" Drake snapped at my Pack brother, and before I could help it a growl escaped my lips. "Shut the bitch up" he warned Gavin – but Gavin didn't say a word to me.

"Is someone going to explain what's going on here?" I asked, not liking the fact Gavin's arms found themselves around my waist, and Drake was moving closer to Landon with the gun. I prayed that Saxon would get there soon.

"We're taking you, and we're getting out of Louisiana" Drake replied, as Gavin continued to stare at me in a really disconcerting way. "We're going to take the money we stole yesterday, and we're skipping town. Gavin is going to turn me into a Wolf".

"He can't Turn you" Landon spoke up, and I sent him a glare telling him to stop talking.

"Why not?" Drake demanded, as Gavin moved forward and brushed his face into my neck. He let out a soft growl, as he buried his face in my nape, and inhaled my scent deeply. I let him do it, because I cared more about Landon than the murderous cannibal pressing his nose into my neck. I yelped in shock when his teeth bit into my neck. Blood spurted over my shirt.

"Chelsea" Landon screamed, voice full of worry. I knew what Gavin was doing, marking his bitch, but I was not happy with it. I was sick of playing nice. I kicked into action. I pushed Gavin away with all my strength, and he flew across the room.

Drake yelped in shock, and Landon took the opportunity to run at him. He knocked the gun out of Drake's hand, and pushed the human to the floor – hard enough that his head bounded off the coffee table. He stayed down, dizzy for a while.

Gavin was a different story. He was up in a second and dived at me. We both hit the floor, with him on top of me. "You're mine" he snarled angrily as he pinned my hands to the ground. He had almost double my strength, and it drove me insane. I was a lot faster, but his strength was even greater than Saxon's.

"This is familiar" Landon muttered, as he shot over in my aid. His foot made contact with Gavin's head and he went down. I pounced to my feet, and the two of us dived on Gavin to hold him to the ground.

For a moment, I thought it was all over. We had Gavin, and we could take care of him and it would all be sorted. But then I heard it, the sound of metal hitting the table. My head spun quickly, to see Drake pulling the gun out from under the coffee table.

"Let him go. Now" Drake demanded, cocking the gun to the side. I cussed. "What dirty language for such a pretty girl" he purred. "Now, let him go and move away from him" he instructed. I growled in annoyance, and Landon mirrored the sign.

But we both comply. We can heal from a lot, but a bullet wound to the head or heart would definitely kill us. We moved away from Gavin, and the bastard stood up and moved to Drake's side. "You, negro, get on the ground" Drake snapped at Landon.

I growled deeply, "watch you language. Don't say shit like that around me, or I'll rip your fucking throat out". I bared my teeth at him.

"Easy beautiful" Drake laughed, amused by my anger. Landon frowned, not liking the name either, but begrudgingly got to his knees. Neither of us could fight guns. All I kept thinking was; *where the hell is Saxon?*

Once Landon was knelt down, Gavin grabbed a thick piece of rope – which from the scent Gavin had used to hold Lauren Powers the night before. Gavin bound Landon's hands around the radiator pipe. Landon would be able to break the rope easily, which I was glad about.

"He'll break through this easily" Gavin stated to Drake. The human sighed, annoyed, before swivelling his gun and shooting at Landon twice. I screamed, as the smell of blood splattered the room.

I dived forward, but Gavin lunged at met me in the air. He kicked me back down, and by the time I stood up the gun was back pointing at me. Landon was crying in pain, and I let out a sigh of relief to see the two bullets had been focused on his shoulders. He had a bullet in each shoulder – painful as hell, but non-lethal.

"Now beautiful" Drake smirked, "we better get going. We're got a long drive to Texas ahead of us". He gestured for me to walk towards the back door, where I could see a long fire escape leaning down to the back street.

I didn't move, so Gavin growled and pushed me on. "Chelsea" Landon cried out, wincing in pain. I sent him one wishful look, before leaving with two psychopathic murders at gunpoint.

Chapter Twenty Seven

Drake drove, with Gavin and I in the back seats. The Forced Turn sat as close to me as possible, with his arms holding me tightly and his face pressed into my neck. The bite wound had stopped bleeding, but with the way his teeth kept nicking at my skin, it would soon reopen. My hands were bound behind my back, with copper wiring, meaning I couldn't push him back.

"You could have any girl, why me?" I growled out. I felt sick to my stomach, but I knew that angering Gavin would get me know where. I had to wait until they got complacent with me, and then kill the both. Or at least kill Gavin, and hand Drake over to the police.

"Mate" Gavin growled out, pressing his face further into my face. I then realised why it was me that Gavin had such an interest in. He was running on Wolf instincts – hunt, eat, mate. I was the only She Wolf in the US, so I was the only one he would consider worthy to mate with.

I shivered at not only his skin on skin contact, but also of the thought of what they planned to do to me. "I was happy to leave you behind, and pick up some more girls along the way. But Gavin was convinced that we needed you, and so we made sure to get you. And I'm sure once he Turns me, I'll think the same" Drake replied.

"So you're just going to give everything up, in the chance to become a Werewolf?" I demanded, as one of Gavin's hand caressed my upper thigh. Bile rose into my mouth, and I swallowed it down.

"Of course. I'll have strength, and speed, and no one would ever be able to fuck with me" Drake replied, as Gavin's hand began to rise.

"Look at Gavin. He's evil. He used to be a good man, a cop and--"

Drake cut me off with a bitter laugh. "A good man? I'm guessing you didn't know Gavin before you bit him, huh?" he laughed again, and even Gavin chuckled against my neck. "You think that girl last night was the first one? Because we do this every summer".

My heart thumped wildly, and I pushed the bile down again. "Gavin was a killer before we Turned him?" I asked, trying to stay calm.

"Killer no? He went a step further last night that normal, but it's not the first time we've had our fun with girls before. If we get a chance, I'll show you all the home made videos we've made" Drake chuckled, his voice making my blood run cold.

"Have your fun with girls? You mean you rape helpless women, and film it" I growled out, fury obvious in my tone. Gavin pulled out of my neck, and growled deeply. Not being able to help myself, I growled back.

Gavin back handed me across the face, and my face stung. My hands fought against the copper wiring, which bound them, but it would take a while for me to break through it. But I knew that the more I fought, the more I would be beaten. So I shut up instantly.

"Gavin doesn't like girls that argue too much" Drake laughed, as Gavin's head went back into my neck. I wished he would stop doing that; he was trying to claim me and I hated having his scent all over me. The only man's scent I wanted over me was Saxon.

"And what do you like, Drakel?" I snapped, trying to keep the growl out of my mouth.

"I like girls who do a lot of pleading". The smile in his voice was obvious, and I cringed awkwardly. I hated them, I hated them more and more with each passing moment. Bloodthirst oozed from my body, and all I wanted to do was kill them – in the most painful and violent way possible.

Gavin's hand ran up my thigh again, and I gritted my teeth. Instead of nuzzling my neck, Gavin turned to kissing my neck. His lips sloppy and wet, trailing hard and aggressive kisses over my skin. His hands moved from my thigh, and they both ran over my stomach.

My hands fought against the wire bound, and I could feel it cutting into my skin. Gavin's hands cupped my breasts, and I couldn't hold the growl off anymore. "She getting feisty back there?" Drake laughed, as Gavin's hands molested me and squeezed my chest. It was such a contrast to the sweet touches of Saxon the night before.

"Get your hands off me, dick" I hissed at Gavin. He slapped me across the face again, lips not even moving from my neck. I was pushing all my strength into breaking the restraints on my hands.

Suddenly, Gavin yanked his face from my neck. "I want her now. Stop the car" he instructed Drake. His voice was gruff and hoarse – the words forming in the very back of his throat.

"We've only been driving for an hour, Gav, the others will catch up" Drake replied, "keep it in your pants until we at least get out of Louisiana".

"No. I want her now" Gavin growled.

"Look, if we wait we can get a motel room, and there will be more room to make sure it hurts". At his words, Gavin growled once more – the second time full of arousal and satisfaction. Drake laughed. "Exactly, man, it will be so much better when we can make her scream".

Gavin looked at me, eyes full of shiny lust. The look disgusted me, and I growled again. Gavin just laughed, before he moved away from me slightly. I was confused at first, before I began to panic when he began to unbutton his jeans.

"Don't you fucking touch me" I snapped at him, hands still pushing against the wire.

"Hey, man, we agreed we'd do it together and film it. Don't ruin it now" Drake called back. Gavin glared in his friend's direction.

"I'm not ruining anything" he snapped, baring his teeth in a primal manner. Gavin turned back to me, as he got his erection out of his jeans. I groaned in disgust, as he began to pleasure himself as he stared at me.

I turned away, tears blurring my vision. I would never let them see my unshed tears, but everything they were saying was bringing up bad memories. I had been through what they wanted to put me through before, and I didn't want to do it again. I had never been treated nicely by men, and then I met Saxon.

I had finally found a man who treated me right – who knew exactly who I was, and what I was, and never once cared. He cared for me, possibly loved me, more than any man ever had in my life. And just when things were going good, I found myself in the grips of more assholes.

When I heard Gavin groan, and I was covered with sticky white ejaculation, I felt my bottom lip quiver. But I took a deep inhale of air, and pushed my emotions away. I could cry all I wanted when I was back with Saxon and Landon, and the rest of the Pack. But right then, I needed to be the strong bitch I knew I was.

I couldn't wipe away Gavin's disgusting fluid, but even if my hands weren't bound I would have left it there. Because if I wiped it away that would give them both the satisfaction of knowing how uncomfortable and upset I was. So I just sat there, eyes staring out the window, as I carried on fighting against my wire handcuffs.

Drake turned to look at me, and laughed manically when he saw me. "Now that really is your colour, beautiful" he roared in amusement. My jaw set, and I bit my tongue.

"You want to claim her?" Gavin asked, and I held back a whimper.

"Hell yeah" Drake yelled, pulling the car to the side of the road. As the two swapped seats, so that Drake was in the back with me, I let a tear out. It slid down my face, but luckily was gone by the time the human was next to me.

Gavin started the car up again, and I was thrown forward as he jerkily pulled the car away and hit the gas as hard as possible. My head hit off the seat in front, and I hissed in pain. Gavin drove like behaved – like a colossal asshole with a death wish.

"Look at me, beautiful" Drake whispered into my ear, as I heard his fly unzip. I swallowed my disgust, but refused to look his way. Annoyed, Drake gripped my chin and snapped my head to look at him. I growled in warning, and Gavin growled back.

"Screw you" I hissed angrily at Drake, before spitting in his face. Gavin growled in fury, but his foot didn't ease off the gas even slightly. Drake, on the other hand, just laughed and wiped his face off.

"No, beautiful, I'm going to screw you".

"You're a pathetically weak human. And the moment I get out of these restraints, I'm going to kill you so painfully, that you'll be the one screaming and begging me to stop. You're nothing Drakel, nothing".

Drake laughed again, as his hands took his own erection out of his jeans. I turned away, once more feel disgusted. I knew why they were doing it – to humiliate and belittle me. And worse than that, it was working.

Drake took the torture one step further, raising himself to his knees, he shoved his throbbing erection into my face. I growled and whipped my head to the side. "Get that tiny thing away from me, or I'll bite it off and lead you to bleed out".

Drake laughed, before he emptied himself over my neck and hair. I couldn't help but whimper that time. Gavin had been over my clothing, but Drake had actually claimed my skin. My hair was fused together and my neck covered in Gavin's kisses and Drake's liquids.

I was so humiliated, that I could no longer hold the tears off. They were silent, but Drake saw them. Two stray tears fell from my eyes, and streaked my face. Drake laughed, as he put himself back in his jeans, with a smug smile.

"That was just a taste of what is to come, beautiful" he laughed, before winking at me.

Chapter Twenty Eight

After almost a day of driving, we arrived in Texas. I was still covered in sticky shit, and when Gavin realised I was breaking through the wire, he secured them. The reason they went to Texas was because Drake's parents – who were abroad – had a large ranch there.

The ranch was in the middle of nowhere; and Drake used the typical 'no one will hear you scream' line. I rolled my eyes at him, as he pulled the car down the long drive way. The Greenall Ranch, was large and brightly coloured.

The sun was setting behind the Ranch, sending a red glow over the ground. Drake stopped the car, and opened my car door. When I didn't move, Gavin gave me a push. I gritted my teeth, but got out of the car.

Drake grabbed my arm, and pulled me close to him. "Wait" Gavin called, as he got out the car. "She's loosened the wire again". Grabbing my hands, he tightened the binding. I yelped in pain when the copper dug into my already red raw wrists.

The sun beat down on us, calling up sweat over my entire body. I hadn't eaten since breakfast, and was still recovering from being beaten by Gavin three days before, so the heat instantly made me light headed.

"Easy there" Drake laughed, steadying me.

"She needs food" Gavin grumbled, as he pushed me in the direction of the house. I groaned as my feet dragged. My vision blurred for a moment, and my head went light. I tried to calm myself, as they pushed me on.

"Hello?" a voice called out to us. "Hey, who's there?"

"I forgot about the ranch hand" Drake mumbled, as we turned to look at the owner of the voice. I had once read an erotic novel about a Texan ranch hand, and looking at him, I could understand. He was beautiful.

He had tousled brown hair, with golden smooth skin and bright green eyes. His body was heavily built up – and as he was shirtless everything was on show. He had a pair of jeans low on his hips, and a cowboy style hat on his head. He extremely tall, at least six foot seven, and towered over all of us.

"Drake, is that you?" he asked, as he reached us. He shot Drake a bright smile, before he glanced at Gavin and then me. When he looked at me, his smile faltered. I bet I looked a sight. Hands bound, swaying in the heat, covered in dried come and blood trailing down from my neck. "Drake what the hell is going on here?" he voice wavered.

Drake was quick, pulling the gun from his belt and pointing it at the ranch hand. "I'm sorry about this Nathaniel, but this is the way it has to be" he said, and the ranch hand's heart rate soared. "Get in the house".

Nathaniel held his hands up slowly, and looked at me with soft eyes. He walked into the house, and Drake grabbed my arm and pulled me after him. "Down to the cellar" Drake instructed Nathaniel.

"Look man, you don't need to do this. Just let me, and the girl go, and I'm sure we can sort all this out" Nathaniel tried to reason with him.

"There is no point trying" I said, as Drake and I walked alongside Nathaniel. "But as soon as they slip up, I'm going to rip both their throats out with my teeth". I growled heavily. Nathaniel looked at me, shocked, before nodding softly.

Drake pulled us down to a wine cellar, which was empty except for a rickety bed. I gulped, knowing exactly what he wanted to use that bed for. He saw my eyes, and confirmed my thoughts. "Soon I'll have you screaming into that bed" Drake whispered into my ear. Nathaniel still heard, and he gulped.

Gavin came up behind us, and gave the ranch hand a hard push. Nathaniel yelped as he fell to the floor from the force. Drake pushed me down too, and I fell next to him. They both made a move to leave. "Please" I begged, making them both pause. "I need to food. I have to eat".

The two shared a look, before Gavin and Drake nodded. They both headed back up the stairs, before returning seconds later. Drake threw me a bottle of water, and three boxes of cookies. They slammed the unbreakable steel door behind them.

I turned to Nathaniel who still looked shocked by Gavin's strength, and the general situation he found himself in. "Hey can you take these off?" I asked Nathaniel, turning so my bound hands were in front of him.

There was a pause, before his hands began to untie the copper wire. I grimaced a few times, due to my wrists already bleeding, but stayed deathly still. Finally, he removed them and my hands were freed. "Thank god" I whispered, shaking my hands out.

I turned back around to Nathaniel and gave him a shy smile. "Are you alright?" he asked, as I grabbed the bottle of water and gulped some down. I wasn't sure when I would next be fed, so only took a little bit.

"No. But hopefully I can get the jump on them when they get down here" I replied, as I ripped open a box of cookies.

"They have a gun. Not to mention that other guy is scarily strong".

"He's a Werewolf" I told him, through a mouthful of cookies. Nathaniel looked at me with disbelief. "I know how it sounds, but he is. Just like I am. Drake isn't, he's just a prick with a gun. But they're both dangerous".

Nathaniel removed his hat, and leant against the wall. I scooted until I sat next to him, and offered him a cookie. He declined. "We don't know when we'll next be fed. Take some" I reminded him. He tenderly picked one up.

I talked him through the basics of Werewolves, and he allowed me to talk and explain the situation. He didn't look like he believed me though. "Can you turn into a Wolf so I can see?" he asked, after I finished talking. I had eaten an entire box of cookies, but he'd barely touched his one.

"I can't. It takes a lot of energy out of me, and I need to keep all the strength I have to fight Drake and Gavin" I explained. He nodded, as if he understood.

"All over you is that…"

"Yeah" I nodded, and he cringed. "I'm the only She Wolf in the US, so Gavin wants to make me his mate. Hence the kidnapping. However, my Sire and my Pack brother will hopefully be able to find us".

"How? You said you were in New Orleans".

"My Sire is a computer genius. He'll quickly be able to find out that Drake's parents own a ranch. Not to mention, he was stupid enough to mention – in front of my Pack brother – that he was taking me to Texas. So it shouldn't be too long".

"Long enough" Nathaniel grumbled, not happy. Just as he said that, the door to the cellar opened, and both Drake and Gavin came down the stairs. They came down, set up a tripod and a camera, which pointed towards me, and pressed play – the camera capturing Nathaniel and I.

Drake pointed the gun at me. "Get up".

"No, shot me" I replied. He sighed heavily, before the gun swung to Nathaniel's direction. The large man bristled at the challenge, but looked terrified.

"You know you can heal from a bullet. But Nathaniel here doesn't stand a chance of survival" Drake replied, with a sardonic smirk.

"Stop all of this. I want her. Now" Gavin shouted from behind. There was a wildness to his eyes again, and his lips were pulled back in a permeant snarl. Drake looked at me, before waving his gun slightly – Nathaniel gulped deeply.

I got to my feet, and Gavin was in front of me in a second. "No, don't touch her" Nathaniel snapped. Both of them ignored him. Even when he jumped to his feet, Drake just moved the gun closer. Nathaniel cussed, but didn't move closer.

Gavin gripped my hand, dragging me towards the bed. As soon as we started moving, I struck. My leg swung out, hitting Gavin's stomach with hard impact. Gavin groaned in pain, and he released me. As he did so Drake snapped his head in our direction.

Nathaniel took the opportunity to strike himself. He dived forward, knocking Drake to the floor with his weight. Drake screamed in pain, and he squeezed his trigger finger. A bullet flew out and hit Nathaniel in the thigh – he went down with a yelp of pain, and the scent of blood filled the air.

In that time, Gavin recovered and dived on me. The two of us went down, my head hitting off the concrete ground, and my own blood spilled out. Kicking out with my leg, I launched his body off me – and he sailed through the cellar.

Nathaniel, still screaming in pain, pushed his body across the floor and grabbed the gun. He shot Drake as he tried to get up. A single bullet pierced Drake's temple – an instant kill, which was exactly what we needed.

Gavin roared in outrage and dived at Nathaniel. With a hard kick to the head, Nathaniel went unconscious. He slumped against the cellar wall, and I felt sorry for him. Gavin rounded on me.

"Finally a rematch" I stated, crouching into a primal fighting position. I could feel the blood dripping down my head, but didn't wipe it away. I looked into Gavin's crazed eyes, and I knew that he didn't care about having a mate any longer. He was going to kill me, and then he would have his way with me.

But I would not allow that to happen again. He had beaten me once, and left me for dead. I was determined to beat him the second time. Gavin was evil, and wicked, and he deserved to die just like his partner in crime.

Gavin made the first move; diving at me. I met him in the air, and we collided with force. We hit the floor, and I used my speed to roll onto of him. I grabbed his neck, my fingers digging into the skin as I straddled him.

Gavin reached up, and with a hard shove he pushed me off him. I rolled along the floor, and my skin scraped against the floor. Gavin dived on me, grabbing my head and slamming it into the floor again. I screamed, and my vision blurred. He really needed to stop doing that – it hurt like a bitch.

Gavin grabbed my head once more, but before he hit my head, I swung my fist into his face. His head snapped to the left, and his grip weakened. I broke out of his hold, and sloppily jumped to my feet. I wobbled on my feet, using the wall to steady myself.

Gavin began to get up, but I swung out a strong roundhouse kick – just like Ernie had taught me – and slammed him back to the ground. Knowing speed was my best defence, I kicked him once more. My boot made contact with his head, and blood spurted with a satisfying squelch.

But despite that, Gavin jumped to his feet. His fist flew at me, and I ducked. I threw my own fist, and he ducked. He danced forward, and I danced back. Both of us were so equally matched, that it made it hard to say who would win. I prayed it would be me, but I couldn't be certain.

Gavin dived at me once more, and I met him with a kick to the stomach. But it wasn't strong enough to stop him, and he knocked me to the ground. His heavy body landed on top of me, and his hands wrapped around my neck.

I choked, struggling to breath, as his fingers constricted my airway. Just as my vision began to spot, a loud gunshot ran out. Gavin's wild, hazel eyes looked into mine, before they rolled back and he went limb on top of me.

As soon as the pressure to my neck left, I sucked in a deep breath. The fresh air hurt to take in, but it was so needed that I didn't care. I coughed like a chain smoker, as I heaved Gavin's head body off me.

Nathaniel looked at me, from where he was slumped against the wall, smoking gun in hand. "Thank you" I breathed out, as I shakily got to my feet. I turned to look around the room, before limping over to the camera. "That's a wrap" I mumbled, before flicking it off.

Chapter Twenty Nine

I helped Nathaniel up the stairs, before placing him down on the couch. "How am I going to explain this to Drake's parents?" he asked, as I grabbed a bottle of scotch from the cabinet.

"You're not" I said, as I knelt in front of him. I grabbed his jeans, and ripped them easily. I then took a heavy swig of the scotch, offered Nathaniel a swig, before using it to disinfect the wound.

Nathaniel cussed and screamed, but didn't complain. I cleaned the wound thoroughly, took another swig myself, before using a set of tweezers to remove the bullet. I then tied a shirt around the wound. "Now what?" he asked.

"Saxon should be here soon. And he'll be able to put stitches in it".

"I didn't mean with my wound" Nathaniel replied, with a small frown.

"Saxon is going to bite you. If you survive you'll become like us, if not you'll be buried like the other bodies downstairs" I told him bluntly.

"Don't bury me with murdering rapists" Nathaniel snapped, most offended by that.

"I would never" I replied, "plus you'll survive, so it won't come to that". I shook my head at him, as the sound of a car turning onto the ranch driveway. My ears perked up, and I sighed heavily. "They're here".

A few minutes later, Saxon's car tore down the ranch entrance and skidded to a stop. Saxon ripped the door open, and was out the car and in front of me in a second. I threw myself at him, and his arms were around me in a second. "I've got you, I've got you" he whispered.

Just being in his arms once more, had warmness spreading through my stomach and my heart beat faster. I broke down in tears, sobbing heavily into his strong muscled chest. I loved him so much that I couldn't help but break down – because being with him meant I was officially safe.

"I've got you, I've got you, I've got you" Saxon carried on whispering into my ear. I pulled back so I could see him, and smiled up into his beautiful speckled gold eyes. Leaning down he pressed a heavy, long, kiss onto my lips.

"I love you" I told him when we pulled away. He pressed a kiss to my forehead, before his chin rested on the top of my head.

"I love you too" he told me, and happiness flooded my body. Moving away, he held me at arm's length and inspected my body. "I can smell them all over you. They didn't...did they?"

"No, just over me" I commented, gesturing to my disgusting sticky appearance. Saxon breathed out in relief, before quickly kissing me again. I moved away and turned to Landon, who stood awkwardly next to Saxon. I hugged him tightly, and he pressed a kiss to my cheek.

I took them inside, and introduced them to Nathaniel. "You saved Chelsea, and for that, I can never repay you" Saxon told him, clasping his shoulder in gratitude. "But you understand what I have to do?"

"I understand" Nathaniel nodded. "Just promise me, that if I don't survive the bite, you won't bury me with them downstairs".

"You have my word" Saxon nodded, offering Nathaniel a small smile.

First, Saxon stitched up Nathaniel's injury as Landon went out to get food and drink. I ventured into the rest of the house, and found one of the many bathrooms. I striped my clothes off, leaving them in a pile to burn later. I turned the shower on, and slipped inside.

Ten minutes later, when Drake's and Gavin's scents were scrubbed off my body, the door opened and Saxon slipped into the bathroom. I offered him a small smile, as he stripped his clothes off, and I opened the door for him to join me.

He closed the door behind him, as I threw my arms around his neck. "I love you" I told him again, as I cuddled into him. His large hands rested on my shapely hips.

"I love you so much" he replied, and I pulled away to kiss him. The kiss started off slow, and delicate, but quickly became heated. Our lips battled heavily, as our tongues tangled. Saxon's fingers dug into my hips, so that I rocked against his hardening member. He moaned into my mouth.

Saxon broke the kiss, as he rested his head against mine. "If you're not ready we don't need to have sex now. You've been through a lot, and they touched you and violated you and--"

"It's not the first time it's happened to me, Saxon. When I was eighteen I was dating this guy, and he was violent. And when I tried to break up with me, he beat me up and raped me. I went to the police, but they didn't believe me because he was my boyfriend, and they basically said it wasn't rape because we were dating".

"Bastards" Saxon whispering, pushing my dark hair backwards.

"I've been through a lot of shit, Saxon. I'm damaged and broken, and I don't know if I'll ever be mended. I'm a lot to take on, so if you don't want to be with me, I understand".

Saxon kissed me; a long, passionate kiss. "If this is you broken, I don't want you mended. I love you as you are, and I don't want you to ever change. I'm all in, Chels".

I leant my head against his, "yeah me too". Our lips battled heatedly, as my arms wrapped around his neck. Saxon picked me up, and my legs wrapped around his waist, as my back pressed against the shower wall. And I was reminded exactly how much he loved me.

An hour later, I curled up with Saxon on the couch. Landon had returned with seven pizzas and we had eaten all of them except one. Nathaniel had a few slices, but watched in shock as the three of us – mostly me – devoured all the pizzas in about ten minutes.

I sat practically on Saxon, and his arms were tightly wrapped around me. "Can we go home after Nathaniel is Turned?" I asked Saxon, as his fingers ran up and down my thigh. I shivered at the contact.

"Yes. My father is due home at the end of the week, so we'll head up there" he nodded.

"Where is the Pack house?" Landon asked, around a mouthful of Meat Feast.

"Rural Alaska" he replied, and even my eyebrows raised. Landon groaned in annoyance.

"Shit, I hate the cold. Does it snow in Alaska this time of year?"

"It snows in Alaska most of the year" I deadpanned, and Saxon chuckled.

After we'd all eaten, we all headed to bed. Saxon, Landon and I shared the spare room, Nathaniel stayed in his own room. When I woke up the following morning, I felt better than I had in weeks.

We started the day with cold pizza, before Landon and I used Nathaniel's truck to move Drake and Nathaniel's bodies. We drove them about an hour away, before burying them in a thick woodened area.

While we were out, Saxon bit Nathaniel. As we were driving back, Nathaniel went into the fever. I was glad – I liked Nathaniel and I really, really, wanted him to survive. He had saved my life, and I would forever be in his debt.

Landon and I stopped at a gas station, and cleaned ourselves off in the bathrooms – I had mud under my nails, and caked onto my hands. Once we looked somewhat presentable, Landon and I headed over to the truckers diner connected to the gas station.

"He really loves you" Landon said, when we scanned the menu.

"I know" I smiled, "he loves you too, Landon. In a different way, but we both love you just as much". My words were met with a bright smile that warmed my heart. Landon was my best friend, and I didn't want him to think that just because Saxon and I were officially together, that our relationship was going to change. Because it wouldn't, not even slightly.

"Alright come on then, Chelsea, does he know how to use those eight inches or not?" he asked, and I choked on a laugh. "Is that the noise you make when you have to deep throat him?"

"You're awful" I laughed, my cheeks hurting because I was smiling so brightly.

"You can't date the sex god that is Saxon Henderson, but not give me details. That is basically a criminal offense".

"Alright, he is one of the best I've ever had".

"Not the best?"

"Well not yet. He has potential, but he's still a bit reserved. Once I bring out his freaky side I'm pretty sure he'll be the best". I waggled my eyebrows, and Landon chuckled. "We've only had sex twice, and both time it was amazing don't get me wrong, but they were both rushed. Hopefully we'll get more time together at the Pack house".

"And just think, it'll be so cold in Alaska. So you'll have to take all your clothes off so that you can share body heat, and you'll have to cuddled up under a sheep skin and--"

"Alright Mr Horny. I think you need to get laid" I giggled. My phone chimed and I smiled when I saw the text from Saxon. "Nathaniel survived the fever".

Chapter Thirty

Stretching my hind legs out, I let out a long groan. I then straightened up, and shook my fur out, as I got accustomed to my new form once more. The sun was setting on the Texan ranch, but the temperature had not cooled any.

Pivoting on my back legs, I saw that Nathaniel and Landon still had a while left of their Shifts. They were younger than me, meaning they weren't as practiced. Saxon had completed his own Shift before me, and padded over as I sat back down on the floor.

Saxon ran his muzzle over my sides, as he walked around me – as if checking me. I couldn't help but shiver when he rubbed his muzzle over my rear. I growled lowly, and Saxon reacted the noise. Neither of us would take our physical relationship past the human boundary, but we could still have fun and flirt.

When he was happy with his scent check, he lay down next to me. I rested my head on his back, as we watched Nathaniel and Landon complete their Shifts. Landon finished first; collapsing to the ground with a moan of pain.

His tongue hung out the edge of his mouth, as Nathaniel screamed into clenched teeth. I pitied him; the more that I Shifted, the less it hurt. It still felt like torture, but I was no longer water board torture it was now just plain stabbing torture.

When Nathaniel had finished his second ever Shift, he collapsed into a heap on the floor. Tenderly I got to my feet, and slowly walked over. His bright green eyes stared at me, as I moved next to him.

He whined softly, and I barked a laugh at him. I then ran my tongue over his sweaty fur, trying to smooth down the erect strands – but it was to no avail. I gave up eventually, and simply sat down in front of him, until he was recovered.

When he finally got his feet, his legs shaking, I barked at him before nuzzling his neck. He growled in happiness as I did so, as he sniffed my scent thickly. When I pulled away from him, Nathaniel growled and jumped at me playfully.

I swatted his muzzle away with my paw, and a growl rumbled his chest. I gave out a deep laugh, as Saxon walked over to us and battered my nose – playful punishment for hitting Nathaniel. I huffed at him, and all the men rumbled out laughs at me.

I turned on the spot, glaring at all of them playfully. Saxon whimpered in apology and I just growled at him. He took a step forward, to comfort me, but before he got the chance I shot off. I sped into the forest around the ranch, and my Pack brothers all laughed again. Then, they began to chase me.

I darted through the vegetation – branches catching my skin, leaves ruffling my fur and mud covering my paws. I pushed as fast as I could, knowing my speed was my best defence. My Pack brothers were catching me, but I had slowed down to allow them to do so.

Landon was close on my trail; his teeth snapping as he tried to catch my long tail between his teeth. When I felt his teeth scrap the tip, and his breath blowing over my hind, I pushed myself faster and sped away.

Landon roared in frustration, and both Nathaniel and Saxon mirrored him. I darted to the left, the move so fast that when Landon tried to copy he skidded on his back feet and crashed into a tree.

My Sire roared out a laugh, as I couldn't help but glance over my shoulder to see him. Landon had landed face down, with his legs up in the air – like a slapstick cartoon who had become stuck in a rabbit hole as they flailed their legs around helpless. I barked a loud laugh at the scene.

Landon gave a mighty screech of anger, and scrambled back to his feet. Saxon and Nathaniel had overtaken him, and caught up with me in the time I had spent laughing at Landon. So I faced the correct way again, and pushed myself on faster.

The boys and I played, and wrestled, for hours – then we hunted. Little wildlife was situated in the forest, but Saxon managed to catch a deer, and he shared it with us. I was still a ridiculously messy eater; and all three boys mocked me for it. I huffed, and we began to wrestle once more.

When the sun was coming up, we finally all Shifted back. "That really is amazing" Nathaniel grinned, as we walked back through the ranch. "And you know, it's so not weird being naked or anything".

"Yeah, I still don't get why a naked body looks different to me now" Landon agreed.

"Because you're running on Wolf instincts" Saxon answered, as I slipped my hand into Nathaniel's. "You know that nudity is normal, and the situation isn't sexual. Just like how you could sleep with Chelsea, or one of your Pack brothers, and it not be sexual or weird. Don't question your instincts, just follow them".

"Except no humping strangers legs or pissing on fire hydrants" Landon smirked, "apparently that's frowned upon".

"No shit" Nathaniel chuckled, as his fingers tightened around mine. "I just can't believe this happened. I mean come on ya'll, things like this don't happen to people like me".

"Me neither" I smiled.

"Nor me" Landon commented, from my other side.

"Well it has" Saxon announced, moving in between Nathaniel and I, and placing his arms around us – his right hand stretching over Nathaniel to rest on Landon's shoulder. I cuddled into his side, our bare skin brushing together. "And it's all about to get a bit more hectic. As soon you'll meet all your other brothers".

Back inside the house, we all quickly showered, before we ate all the food left in the pantry. "So I can marry a human, then?" Nathaniel asked, as we cuddled on the couch. Saxon and Landon had gone out to collect supplies for our long trip, and refuel the car.

"You can marry whoever you fall in love with" I replied, as I sipped on a beer.

His hand skimmed my bare thigh, "this isn't sexual right? Because usually when I sit with a girl practically on my lap, wearing only a shirt and underwear, I'm normally turned on. But I don't feel anything".

"This isn't sexual. I'm with Saxon, and I love him very much. Wolves show affection through touch. Humans won't understand that, but that is how it is. We are cuddling because we share a strong platonic love".

"So if I fell in love with a She Wolf, I could marry them?"

"You could. But it's unlikely you will meet another She Wolf. There is only five of us worldwide, and I'm the only one in the US" I explained, "so it's more likely you'll settle down with a human girl".

"And I can tell her about what we are?"

"Only after you marry. But I don't know about telling your family, I don't know what the rules are on that. You'll have to ask Saxon". I took another sip of my beer, and Nathaniel did the same – his thoughts analysing everything I had told him.

"So you and Saxon are pretty serious then?" Nathaniel asked, after a few minutes of silence.

"I guess. We've not really had time to talk about things. I mean, we've only slept together twice. When we get to the Pack house, we will hopefully be able to spend more time together and just clarify things between us".

When Saxon and Landon returned, they had brought us more food. After eating, Nathaniel was beginning to fall asleep from exhaustion. He headed off to bed, and the rest of us finished off packing his stuff for him – and we placed them in the back of his truck.

I climbed into bed with Landon, and Saxon shared with Nathaniel; as he still wanted to keep an eye on Nathaniel's transition to Werewolf. I slept on my best friend's hard chest, and dreamt of Gavin and Drake as I did so.

The following morning, we all set off. Landon rode with Nathaniel, in his truck, and I drove Saxon's car with him riding shotgun. We had a long drive ahead of us, and I couldn't help but be excited that I would be spending the time with the man I loved most in the world.

"Saxon?" I asked, about three hours into the drive. He made a noise, to indicate he was listening to me. "What are we?"

Saxon looked confused, "what do you mean?"

"Not to sound completely neurotic and obsessed. I don't want you dating anyone else" I stated. Saxon was silent for a long while.

"You think I would date someone else?"

"No, I don't think you would. But I just want to put it out there. I love you, Saxon, you know I do. And I don't want to be hurt anymore. So, I just need you to tell me exactly where I stand".

"You don't stand anywhere, Chels. You're everywhere and you're everything" he replied, reaching over and placing his callous palm on my thigh. "I don't say 'I love you' lightly. I've only ever told one other girl those words, and I didn't feel as strongly about her as I feel about you. You can put a label on us if you want, but it won't ever change my intentions".

"But I could tell people you're my boyfriend?"

"You can tell people I'm your mate if you want" he shrugged, a soft blush on his cheeks. I gave him a confused look – I knew what a mate was, but I didn't understand it in his context. "Wolves mate for life, Chelsea" he explained, and my heart thumped so hard it hurt.

Chapter Thirty One

Three days later, we reached Alaska. There was no snow, which Landon was happy about, but it was still cold. The sun was breaking through the white clouds, casting a soft glow over the shimmering mountains. "It is beautiful" I commented, as Saxon slowed the car down.

"Not as beautiful as you".

"Rule number one of being my mate; no cheesy lines or compliments. They are cringy and I dislike them" I told him, and he laughed warmly.

"Duly noted". He turned the car into a dock, and parked up. Nathaniel's truck rolled in after us. Landon and he jumped from the truck, as we both climbed out. Landon stretched largely, like a cat.

"I've been sat down for too long. I forgot what it was like to have feeling in my ass" he complained, and we all laughed at him. Landon and Nathaniel went and used the restroom, as Saxon and I brought us tickets for the next ferry over to Kodiak Island.

"You kids here for a holiday?" the man asked, as he issued us our tickets.

"No, Sir, we live just outside Larson Bay" Saxon replied, as his arm slipped around my waist and held me to his side. "Some of my family and I are just back for a visit".

"Oh right. Just outside Larsen Bay you say, boy? You ever heard of the Henderson family?"

"We're part of the Henderson family" Saxon replied snappily, and the man gulped. His eyes looked scared, and I quipped an eyebrow at my mate. His hand squeezed my waist, his way of saying he would explain things to me later.

"Oh right, sorry Sir. H-here are your t-tickets. You have a g-good day, sir". The man suddenly reeked of fear, and his hands were shaking slightly. He handed Saxon the tickets – his hands retreating faster than normal.

"Thank you" Saxon replied, a strained smile on his lips.

"Yes, sir. Of course, sir. Have a good day, sir" he rambled. Using his arm, Saxon steered me away and we headed back to the car.

"What was that about?" I whispered.

"I will explain everything when we get on the ferry" he replied, giving my waist a small squeeze. I frowned at him, and he simply pecked my lips gently, before moving away from me to give Nathaniel and Landon their tickets.

"You two head onto the boat, we'll park the cars in the lower decks and meet you at the top" Saxon told Landon and I. We both nodded, and I kissed him quickly once more, before I headed onto the boat with Landon.

The large ferry was dark blue and white in colour, with a small deck on top and a large parking bay that took up the majority of the boat. Climbing the rickety stairs, onto the boat, a tall man stood at the entrance.

He checked our tickets, not looking too happy, but allowed us in. Pressing a hand to my lower back, Landon pushed me on. We moved to the edge of the boat, leaning against the railing, and I pulled my coat closer around me against the sharp wind. We stared out at the water.

"The guy selling us the tickets practically shit himself when he realised we were part of the Henderson family" I whispered to Landon. The deck was quiet, but people were beginning to fill the space.

"What did Saxon say?" Landon asked me. His voice was too loud, so I sent him a glare and he mumbled a quiet apology.

"He snapped at him. He didn't seem happy about him mentioning it".

"Saxon snapped at a stranger? Our Saxon? Our Sire, Saxon? Your boyfriend, Saxon?" he asked in disbelief. I nodded yes. "I don't believe that. I can imagine you snapping at a stranger, but Saxon is the poster child for politeness".

"I know" I frowned, wondering why Saxon had acted so strange when his family had been mentioned. I leant into Landon, and he let me rest my head on his shoulder. We continued to stare out at the choppy water for a few minutes.

When Saxon and Nathaniel met us, the dock was almost full of people. We found a small bit of bench left, so they all squeezed on, and I sat on Nathaniel's wide knee. A few minutes later, the ferry left the dock.

"So what happened with that ticket seller?" I demanded, as the boat caught speed. Saxon leaned in slightly, and we all mirrored his actions – no doubt we looked suspicious, all leaning in like a school gang on a playground.

"So the Pack house is about five miles outside of a small town called Larson Bay. And there, our family have a bit of a…reputation".

"A reputation? Like how in school I was known for accidently pissing myself during dodgeball?" Landon asked. There was a moment of silence.

"No, Landon, nothing like that" Saxon shook his head at him, before carrying on his story. "About forty years ago, one of our Pack members went off the rails, and decided to go after the Pack directly. Naturally, he was killed and his bodied buried. But my father made the mistake of hiding the body too close to the town".

Saxon paused for a moment, clearing his throat. "Then, ten years later, some builders discovered the body. Obviously, people knew he was part of the family, and they questioned us. But there was no ties to us – of course we know what we're doing".

"I still don't understand" I frowned.

"I'm done with the story yet. The police knew it was homicide, so did some looking around. He had a house we didn't know about, on the outskirts of town. I told you he went off the rails, and when he did, he became a man eater but his was out of sadistic pleasure".

"Like sadism?" Nathaniel asked, dark eyebrows pulling together.

"Exactly. The police found bones, and decomposed bodies, in all sort of fucked up ways. And all around the house was evidence of Satan worship – symbols and things. It reflected badly on the entire Pack".

"People thought you were all Satan worshippers and killers" I deduced, and Saxon nodded sadly.

"And thirty years later, and the rumours have just got worse and worse. And now if anything weird happens, instantly it is our fault. And because we do keep to ourselves, and are different to humans, it doesn't help at all. We've had it all; Satan worshippers, witches, cults – the whole lot. I didn't mean to snap at the man earlier, but my entire childhood was ruined because of those rumours. I just lost my temper" he sighed.

Seeing his sadness, I reached up and cupped his cheek. Saxon offered me a small smile, before turning his head and pressing a gentle kiss to my cupped palm. He took my hand in his, and rested them between us.

"So basically if we go out in the town, we have to make sure not to pretend to hex people. No matter how much they piss us off?" I smirked, lightening the mood. Saxon laughed sadly.

"Things are already bad enough, so no, I wouldn't suggest pretending to curse people".

"It'll be worse for me" Landon exclaimed, and we all looked at him. "Being black is bad enough in small towns. But being black and a Satan worshipper is even worse. I might as well just hand them some matches and tie myself to a cross".

"Jesus wasn't black" I snorted.

"I think he meant the Spanish Inquisition" Saxon laughed.

About an hour later, the boat reached the dock and we headed back into the cars. When the ferry was anchored, we followed all the other cars off. Saxon's hands were tight around the steering wheel as he drove.

"Nervous?" I questioned. He pondered that for a moment.

"My father won't arrive until tomorrow, but I'm just worried about Ernie telling him about Gavin before I get a chance too. My father ordered me not to Force Turn anyone, and I ignored his direct order. I'm just…I just want to explain things to him myself".

"I doubt Ernie will have said anything" I assured him, reaching over and giving his thigh a squeeze. "Your father loves you, and cares for you. So don't worry, he'll understand".

"Yeah, but I feel like this was a test. And as soon as he finds out I disobeyed him, he's not going to be happy" he admitted.

"A test? What do you mean?"

Saxon glanced at me, "if I tell you something, you have to swear that you won't tell anyone else in the Pack".

"I swear it".

"Ernie turned down the Dominate position".

"What? When? Why?" I barrelled the questions his way.

"I don't know why, but when my father told us his plans to overthrow the Alpha, Ernie told him that he didn't want to take over as Dominate. And then, suddenly, out of the blue my father is giving me this recruiting job – which he could have given to any of my brothers".

"Maybe he just had the most faith in you".

Saxon snorted unattractively, "no. I know how my father works, this was a test. He sees me as the next trustworthy Pack member after Ernest. So this was a test".

"A test of your skills to become a Dominate" I whispered, understanding what he was getting at.

"Exactly. I think my father was testing me to see if I could take over from him. And I'm pretty sure I just fucked that up". His words were sharp, and I couldn't reply – because I wasn't sure what to say. So I kept quiet, as the car chugged on towards the Pack house.

Chapter Thirty Two

It was early morning when we reached the Pack house. The dark night made the large forest landscape look murkier and more sinister. We drove through a small, winding, road that led us to a large estate – which was spread for about seven thousand acres.

Saxon pulled up at a large iron gate, which stretched around the entire territory. Stepping out of the car, Saxon typed a code into a key pad, before the large gates opened. I drove the car through, and Nathaniel's truck followed. Saxon then typed the code into a keypad on the other side to shut them.

"The code is 1475" he informed us, before he climbed into back into the car. He drove us down the long driveway; we could only see what the headlights showed us. Thick forest surrounded us, and hid the sky above us.

It took us five minutes before we reached the main house. It was large, mansion sized, with a sandy exterior and rows of large windows and looked out into the woodland. There were large sculptures of wolves on either side of the entrance – it was too dark to see the detail, but even from the car I could tell they were professionally sculpted.

Saxon didn't stop the car, he simply drove past the house and down one of the small roads behind the house. Nathaniel's truck paused, before following us further. Two minutes later, we arrived at a small wooden cabin.

Saxon stopped the car, and jogged up to Nathaniel's truck. The Omega rolled his window down, as his Sire approached. "Take the road to the left, it will take you to another cabin about five minutes away. That's one of the guest cabins, and until we actually moved you both into one, you two can stay in there".

"Sure thing" Nathaniel grinned.

"Chelsea and I will come grab you in the morning. It's too late to try and meet everyone now" Saxon told them. We both said goodbye to Nathaniel and Landon, and they drove down to the next cabin along.

"So we get a cabin all to ourselves" I purred, my mind alight with dirty thoughts. Saxon chuckled, as he got our bags from the trunk. "And it'll be cold, so we'll have to take our clothes off to share body heat" I flirted,

Saxon laughed at me, slipping his arm around my waist and pulling me to him. I giggled as I crashed into his broad chest. I kissed him gently, our lips moulding together for the briefest moments of passion.

Pulling away, Saxon's eyes remained closed for a few seconds and he made a primal noise in the back of his throat. "You're so good at that" he groaned, as his eyes slowly opened.

"Come on, let's go inside" I grinned, taking his hand and pulling him towards the cabin. Saxon growled friskily, as I walked backwards and he followed – his arms slipping around my shapely hips.

He pressed me against the cabin door, his lips claiming mine once more. My arms wrapped around his neck, as our lips tangled together. Saxon's hand reached up and sloppily typed in a code to his cabin.

He got the numbers wrong a few times, before finally the keypad beeped, and the door I was pushed up against opened. We fell backward – into the cabin – with Saxon landing on top of me. We both laughed, as his lips moved down to my neck.

"Shut the door, we're letting all the cold in" I giggled, pushing him off me. Saxon groaned in annoyance before getting off me so we could move out of the doorway. He closed the door to the cabin, as I glanced around.

"Alright it's closed, let's remove your clothes and get you warmed up" he growled, diving back down on to me, as his lips claimed mine once more.

"Saxon wait" I giggled, pulling away from him as his kisses moved down to my neck. I pushed him away, and he made a noise of annoyance. I scooted out from underneath him, and stood up.

"No stay on the floor" he groaned, and I chuckled again.

"Let me just see the cabin" I replied, glancing around the room. The cabin was small, and cosy, with a double bed in the centre, and a large closet to the side. A small bathroom was visible from where I stood – and that was all their way. But despite the size, it was homily and comfortable.

A desk stood opposite the bed, with a large computer monitor and ridiculous amount of papers and work surrounding it. Slowly walking over, I noticed all the paper had notes and scribbles on them; all in Saxon's hand.

On the wall above the computer, was a large cork board – with a display of pictures on it. The majority of them were computer related work, for which I didn't understand, but a few were photographs. "This is your cabin exclusively" I commented.

A teenage Saxon was in a number of the pictures; with three other boys. They seemed to be close, as they wore matching shirts in one picture, and costumes in the other ones. I glanced at the pictures closely. "Yeah, go on, laugh. I'm a comic book nerd, who has only ever had three friends outside of his family" Saxon muttered from behind me.

"Laugh? I was actually about to say how cute you looked in these pictures" I replied. Saxon gave a sarcastic laugh, as his hands slipped around me from behind. I leant against him, as I looked at the picture. "I mean, yeah, you were a little skinnier and you had a little more acne" I began, and Saxon snorted. "Alright, a lot skinnier and a lot more acne. But I think it is cute how you're a little bit of a closet star wars geek" I teased.

"That's a star trek costume, Chels, not star wars".

"Same thing" I shrugged, uncaring.

"It most certainly is not" he exclaimed, "star trek is vastly different to star wars. To begin with--" he paused, when he caught my look. "You don't care, got it. You see now why I didn't lose my virginity until I was twenty two?"

I spun in his arms, "what? Seriously? Twenty two?" My words made his blush brightly, and I couldn't help but giggle.

"Yeah. I've only been with one other girl besides you" he shrugged, as my arms wove around his neck. I grinned even brighter.

"That explains so much" I whispered, more to myself than him. But he heard and frowned at me.

"Are you trying to say I'm bad in bed?"

"What? No, not at all. Saxon you're amazing in bed, but you're also…" I trailed off, not sure how to finish.

"Also what?" he prompted.

"Nervous. You hold back a lot, as if you don't really know what you're doing. You're almost scared to give into your emotions too much" I told him. Saxon was quiet for a moment, his blush worsening.

"My last girlfriend – my *only* girlfriend – sort of treated sex like water" he told me, and I quipped an eyebrow in amusement. "More of a necessity than a want. Always missionary and always the same length of time. She knew I wanted it, so we had sex, but I don't think she ever *really* enjoyed it".

"Well I enjoy it" I purred, pressing my body against his. "In fact, I love it. I think about it, dream about it, even fantasise about it". I moved closer, lowering my voice. My breath fanned over his neck, making him shiver. "I love to fuck, Saxon. I love it rough, and hard, and dirty. For me it is not water, it is champagne".

"I want you" Saxon shivered.

"You've got me, Saxon" I whispered, trailing my lips over his jaw. "Tell me what you want me to do, and I will do it. Whatever you want, I will do it right now. Nothing is off limits with me, Saxon. Tell me what you dream of when you're alone Saxon, what you dream of doing to me".

Saxon gulped deeply, as my hand ran down his chest and landed on the bulge in his jeans. "I want you to get on your knees and show me how much you love me" he growled out – a deep lustful tone to his usually smooth voice. I shivered in pleasure.

But, I did as he said. I sunk to my knees in front of him, and looked up into his beautiful gold speckled eyes. "You ever had a blow job before?" I asked him, smirking as I already knew the answer. He shook his head no, obviously both nervous and excited at the same time.

Knowing that Saxon was so inexperienced, and innocent, had me smiling from the inside out. I had a bad habit of being extremely insecure about the man I was dating, cheating on me. But the fact that I could give Saxon all the thing he had dreamt about, but never received, made me feel more confident about myself than ever.

I knew Saxon and I were well matched in our emotional relationship, and knowing I could fulfil his every physical desire, had me believing that we truly could be mates. I loved him deeply, and I knew I could show him that in our physical relationship as well as our emotional.

Reaching up, I slowly unbuttoned Saxon's jeans – allowing them to fall and gather at his ankles. His underwear quickly followed, leaving a hard erection inches from my face. Saxon let out a slow breath, as I looked up into his eyes, before taking him into my mouth.

I put my hands on his hips and began rocking my head back and forward; moving him in and out my mouth. Saxon groaned before he grabbed my head and forced me to take more of his in my mouth. He was big, so I couldn't take him all in my mouth, but I took as much as I could. I rocked back and forward again, closing my mouth as tight as possible around him.

After a while, his erection began to pulse, as he moaned and cussed in enjoyment. I moved away before he could release himself. Saxon let out a noise of annoyance, as I stood up in front of him. I pressed a hot, passionate, kiss to his lips – no doubt he could taste his pre-excitement on my lips.

When I pulled away, we were both breathing hard. I took a step back and removed my shirt, before the rest of my clothes went with it. Saxon grinned, as his practically savagely ripped his own clothing away.

"Tell me how you want to take me" I whispered, taking his hand and pulling him over to the bed. I could see the excitement in Saxon's eyes, making him seem like an excitable teenager rather than a man in his mid-twenties.

"From behind" Saxon breathed out. I came to a stop at the edge of the bed, and turned around to face him.

"On all fours, or against the wall?" I offered, and his eyes shone again.

"The wall" he nodded excitedly, "the wall. Please, the wall". His answer was exactly what I wanted to hear, and I smiled. Turning away, I walked over to the bed next to the wall, and pressed my hands to it, and pushed my ass out and wiggled it at him playfully. Saxon laughed, as he walked up behind me, his hands running over my naked ass.

Teasingly, his fingers slipped inside me quickly. I moaned, as his pushed his finger in and out of me a few times, as he pressed his chest against my back. My head fell back, giving him access to kiss my neck.

When he removed his fingers, he slipped his erection into me straight away. I moaned in pleasure, having forgotten how large and thick he was. I pressed my hands against the wall, to steady myself, as his hands held onto my hips to keep me in place.

Saxon lasted for hours – and that wasn't an exaggeration. We both had the stamina of Werewolves, and we went for hours. Every position Saxon wanted, we did, and I lost track of how many orgasms we had.

But I knew once thing for sure – it was the best sex I had ever had in my life.

Chapter Thirty Three

I awoke in Saxon's arms, our bodies pressed against one another. The cold sun was streaming through the cabin windows, casting an odd glow over the small room. I glanced at the clock, to realise it was close to eight am.

"Saxon" I whispered to my lover, shaking him softly to arouse him. He groaned in his sleep, as his eyes opened slowly. It took him a moment to focus on the situation, before he smiled a beautifully lazy smile.

"Morning baby girl" he said, around a yawn.

"Rule number two of being my mate – no disgustingly cute nicknames" I chuckled.

"Sorry. Good morning, Miss Russell".

I nodded, "much better, Mr Henderson". I leant forward, and kissed his lips gently. He let out a soft groan through my kiss. "We should get up soon. What time are you expecting your father home?" I asked.

Saxon pushed my loose hair behind my ear. "Should get here in about an hour. But my mother, and a few others will be inside. We should meet them first" he told. I made an odd noise, which escaped my mouth before I could stop it. "What was that for?"

"You're the youngest of seven brothers, no doubt your mother will hate any girl you date" I grumbled. Saxon chuckled, as he gave my hip a squeeze, as I glanced up into his eyes. "I'm not exactly the kind of girl most mothers would pick out for their son".

"Yes, she's protective. But once she sees how much I love you, she'll be fine Chels" he smirked, pecking my lips softly. We showered together, before getting dressed. Saxon pulled something clean from his closet, but I only had my clothes that were almost a month old. So I pulled on my last pair of clean jeans, and boots, before taking one of Saxon's cleans shirt and tying it to reveal my toned stomach.

Throwing on one of Saxon's lumberjack style coats, we both headed out the cabin. I slipped my hand into his, as our boots crutched the frozen vegetation. "So I was thinking--"

"Did that hurt?" I smirked, and he pushed my shoulder playfully.

"I was thinking that all your stuff is in my apartment in Toronto anyway. So, when this is all over, maybe we just unpack your things there" he shrugged, his cheeks flaming in embarrassment.

"Well if we unpacked my things there, then all my things would be in your apartment" I replied, playing dumb as I loved watching him blush.

"That is the general idea, yes".

"So if my things are at your apartment then--"

"Chelsea, stop" Saxon groaned, and I laughed warmly. "Please, just move in with me". His words made me smile, and I stopped to kiss him passionately. I pulled back, and Saxon breathed out heavily. "I'm going to take that as a yes".

"I want my own cabin though. I just need my own space occasionally, so I want my own cabin here" I told him, and he happily agreed. We chatted idly about 'our' apartment for a while, before we reached the first guest cabin.

We woke Nathaniel and Landon up, before the four of us walked back to the main house. "You look nervous" Landon commented, as the house came into view.

"She worried about meeting my mother" Saxon informed them, squeezing my hand softly in reassurance.

"Understandable. You're not the kind of girl that people want to bring home to meet their parents" he replied. Saxon sent him a look of annoyance, as Nathaniel snorted in amusement. His words, although true, did nothing to ease to my butterflies.

When we reached the house, we walked up the main stairs, and I eyed the Wolf statues once more. Saxon rung the bell to the main house, and I heard chatted inside. A few seconds later the door swung open.

"Saxon" an older woman – obviously his mother – squealed happily. Mrs Henderson was my height, with shoulder length grey hair and large bright eyes. She had the same ivory pale skin as her son, but hers was chapping with age.

"Hey mum" Saxon smiled, dropping my hand to hug his mother. When he stepped away, he took my hand once more. Mrs Henderson glanced at the touch, and her smile strained as she looked at me. "Mum, this is Chelsea. Chelsea, this is my mother".

"It's lovely to meet you, Mrs Henderson" I said, offering her a shaky hand shake.

"Pleasure" Mrs Henderson replied, her smile straining even more. She then turned to the people behind us. "And who do we have here?" she asked – her voice suddenly happy and her smile genuine.

"My name is Nathaniel, Ma'am, and this is Landon" the youngest Turn replied, showing us all his southern charm.

"Please, call me Katherine. And it's a pleasure to meet you. Come on in, come on in" she waved, beckoning my Pack brothers in. I glanced at Saxon in desperation, feeling deflated and slightly hurt. Saxon offered me a sad smile, before pressing a soft kiss to my temple as we followed the others inside.

"Everyone, Saxon returned with two new Turns" Katherine shouted.

"Three" I corrected her, but she just glared at me. I decided to keep my mouth shut from there on around her.

Saxon just gave my waist a squeeze, as he shut the door behind him. Footsteps echoed through the house, as people headed in our direction.

Saxon pushed us on, and we met the rest of the people in the lounge – a grand room with a red and gold colour theme. Four men walked in; well, three men and a young boy. The men were all Werewolves, and the boy was obviously one of their sons.

"Pup, good to see you" one of Saxon's brothers grinned, stepping forward. Then his eyes zoned in on me, and his smile dropped. "Well, fuck me".

"Albert you watch your language" Katherine scowled her son. Albert was in his mid-thirties, but from his looks, and fashion, he didn't look much older than me or Saxon. He wore a tight black shirt, tucked into a pair of skinny jeans. His dark hair tousled and his jaw sharper than Saxon's – he was definitely the most attractive brother.

"Hello there beautiful" Albert purred, walking up to me and taking my hand. "My name is Albert, and one day you will carry my children". He kissed the back of my hand. Saxon growled in warning, and pushed his elder brother away.

"Watch it, Albie" he warned, arm slipping around my waist.

"Oh come on, pup, don't be so selfish" Albie winked at me playfully.

"Albie, put your dick back in your pants and shut up" a voice from behind him grumbled. Another of Saxon's brother stepped forward. All of them had the same dark hair, dark eyes, and pale skin. However, the eldest brother in the room had an almost feminine edge to him. His hair was quaffed perfectly, his expensive suit was pressed and his face was thinner and more prominent.

He walked up to me and offered me his hand to shake. "Isaac, pleasure to meet you".

"Chelsea" I shook his hand, "and the pleasure is all mine".

"Holy shit, she's British" Albie threw his hands into the air. "I told you I fancy British woman over all over nationalities. This is so unfair, why does Saxon get dibs?"

"Because Saxon doesn't ever say he has 'dibs' over a woman" I replied, and the brothers all snorted. Isaac then introduced himself to Nathaniel and Landon, who politely shook his hand. Isaac had a real corporate vibe to him; like everything was a business deal.

The third brother to introduce himself was Calvin. Calvin looked extremely similar to Saxon, just slimmer and older looking – even though he was the second youngest brother. Calvin shook my hand, almost awkwardly, as he couldn't keep his eyes off me. He wasn't half as awkward with my Sire brothers.

Then came the young boy. "I don't get it" he stated, crossing his arms and looking at me through squinted eyes. "Yeah she's hot, and has massive boobs. But it's not like you haven't fucked hotter girls than her before" he told Albie.

"She's a Werewolf too, kid" Albie told him, and the boy's eyebrows raised.

"What?" Katherine squealed too loudly. She turned to Saxon with angry eyes. "Why didn't you tell me she was a Turn too?" she hissed.

"To be fair, you didn't really give him a chance" I cut in. Her glare intensified on me, before she turned on her heels and stormed out the door. I gave Saxon a desperate look.

"She'll come around" he said, pressing another kiss to my temple – but even when he said it, he didn't sound convinced.

"Not that anyone cares but my name is Caleb" the teenager grumbled, crossing his arms over his slim chest. Caleb was tall and gangly, with the Henderson dark hair but his eyes were a dark green that he obviously got from his mother.

"Caleb is Albie's son. He's sixteen, so has two years until his first Shift" Isaac explained to me. I smiled at him, and he nodded back.

"But he's a bastard child" Albie chimed up, glaring at Isaac. "A young, bastard, mistake. I'm still very single, and very fertile".

"Hey" Caleb exclaimed in annoyance.

"Shut up, you're cock blocking me" Albie hissed to his son.

"Believe me, Caleb isn't the reason your flirting isn't working" I told him, and everyone smirked at Albie. The flirtatious brother opened his mouth to say something else, but I held my hand up to silence him. "I heard the gates open" I told Saxon.

"Wow, you have amazing hearing" Isaac commented.

"My smell isn't up to much though" I replied, as I listened to a car pass through the gate and roll down the driveway.

"Must be dad" Calvin said, glancing at his watch. "Ernie and Allison said they were meeting dad at the ferry about an hour ago. So it should be them". It didn't take long for the car to stop outside the house. Saxon seemed to sense my nervousness, and he took my hand in his.

"Ready to meet your Dominate, Miss Russell?" Saxon asked, smiling softly.

"Ready as I'll ever be".

Chapter Thirty Four

Victor Henderson walked like he owned the world. His shoulders were square, and strong, and his body was the same. His dark hair was greying at the edges, and his eyes had thick wrinkles under them. But even with his age, no one could deny he was a handsome man.

He stepped out the car, his expensive shoes clicking on the gravel and looked over the people in front of him. As soon as his eyes settled on me, they widened a fraction. He took a deep inhale of my scent, before his lips tilted up into a bright smile – making him look almost identical to Albie.

He made a beeline for me, racing fast but never breaking a walk. He stopped in front of me, and I looked up into his dark eyes with a gulp. He looked at me for a long moment, before taking me in his arms in an embrace.

His hug was so warm, and father like, that I couldn't help but wrap my arms around him tightly. It had been so long since I had a hug from someone that resembled anything like a father – and for a moment I got choked up. But I quickly swallowed it, and moved away from him.

"Welcome to the Pack" he smiled, his voice like liquid gold.

"It's a pleasure to be part of it, Sir" I replied, every instinct in me telling me to cast my eyes downwards in submission. But I held his eyes, because I was so warmed by his acceptance.

"Dad, this is Chelsea. She's my mate" Saxon stated, pressing his hand onto my lower back. Victor eyes looked shocked for a moment, before he grinned another wide grin.

"I'm happy for you kids" he said, hugging Saxon in a manly way before pressing a kiss to my cheek. I almost melted when he did so – his acceptance was so heart-warming that my eyes blurred with tears. But once more I just swallowed my emotions, and smiled at my Dominate.

"Thank you, Sir" I said. Victor nodded at me, before turning and introducing himself to Nathaniel and Landon. Once the introductions were done, we all followed Victor inside. Ernie gave me a hug in greeting again, before introducing me to his beautiful red haired wife – Allison. I made an apology for the blood I left in her guest room; she just laughed at me.

"Everyone into the office" Victor bellowed after he walked into the house. Instantly everyone began to move. Katherine gave her husband a kiss before heading into the kitchen, and both Caleb and Allison followed her.

"Chelsea, only the men go into the office" Katherine snapped at me, as I walked towards the office door with the others. I paused glancing at her in confusion.

"No, she comes in. She's part of the Pack" Victor spoke up, placing his hand on my lower back and pushing me in front of him.

"Victor" Katherine exclaimed angrily.

"Later, Kathy, we'll talk about this later" Victor warned her – his tone telling her not to push the subject further. Her jaw set, but she didn't argue with her husband. She stomped into the kitchen, like a small ball of anger. "Ignore her, she's just angry that she isn't allowed in on the meetings" Victor winked at me. I sent him a bright grin.

Victor's office was large; which a mahogany desk and large book shelves that stretched over two of the long walls. There were two cream couches, and two small red love chairs. Victor sat behind his desk. Saxon sat in one love chair, and Ernie moved towards the other – but Victor sent him a look, and he moved to the couch.

There was a moment of pause, as everyone – apart from Saxon and me – looked at Ernie in confusion. Victor waved Isaac to the red seat; the elder brother gulped and took a seat. I realised what had just happened – in turning down the position of Dominate, Ernie had fallen down in the Pack rankings.

"What happened at the rest of the Council Meeting, Sir?" Saxon demanded, as the rest of us sat on the couches.

"Alpha Mashkov is getting worse" Victor sighed, leaning back in his chair. "Luckily for us, the other Dominates didn't have a majority so his most ridiculous ruling didn't pass".

"What ruling was that, Sir?" Isaac asked.

"There was two actually. The first was that he wants to make it illegal to Turn any human into a Werewolf – no matter the situation".

"But surely our numbers are already dwindling already, ruling out the prospect of Turns would reduce the rate that Wolves are reproducing. That means that our race is going to become extinct fifty percent quicker on average" I commented, thinking it stupid. Once I finished speaking, everyone turned to me in shock. "What?"

"Only people in the red seats can interrupt the meeting" Saxon told me, and I think my face flamed redder than his did when I embarrassed him. I was so desperate to prove myself to the Pack, and especially Victor, and my big mouth had fucked that up within minutes.

"I'm sorry, Sir" I apologised, eyes casting downwards to my lap. Victor studied me for a moment, before clearing his throat.

"Isaac sit back on the couch. Chelsea move onto the red seat" Victor said in a clipped voice. I felt my lips tugging into a smile, but I pushed it away. Isaac instantly stood up, and we changed seats. I could feel everyone's eyes on me, and I realised my blush was worsening. "Chelsea, please repeat what you said" my Dominate asked. I did as he asked.

"Surely, he can't expect the race to continue with just Borns" Saxon frowned.

"Plus if a Pack is stronger with a female, then the only way to get a female is by Turn" I added. Victor listened to the two of us, eyes watching us closely – like a teacher observing his students.

"You said that was the first ruling, what was the second one, Sir?" I asked Victor.

"Yes, Chelsea, I did. The second ruling is that he wants to exile all Turns from Packs" he said solemnly.

"What make all Turns Roamers?" Saxon exclaimed, frowning as he looked over at me with worry. Victor nodded yes. "But what about Dominate Gabin of France, he's a Turn. Does that mean demoting him, or kicking him out the Pack completely, Sir?"

"That was one of his questions too" Victor frowned, "Alpha Mashkov said it was to help reduce the work load of Dominates by keeping Pack's within families".

"But surely exiling Turns is just going to double the Dominate's work load" I commented.

"In what aspect?"

"Well if there are more Roamers that means more work for the Packs to keep an eye on them all. And if the Pack numbers are deducing, then surely the Pack will be even more stretched on the number of Wolves being able to enforce the Dominate's rules. Thus meaning more crimes being committed by Roamers and less being disciplined for it".

"Did you just say 'thus'?" Saxon chuckled at me, eyes sparkling.

"Hey, I can be clever sometimes too" I replied, poking my tongue out at him. Victor cleared his throat, and we both muttered apologies before turning back to our Dominate.

"That's a very good point, Chelsea, no one mentioned that in the meeting" he muttered, jotting down my answer in his diary. "Very good" he nodded. I smiled, pride shining out of me – I was so glad that I had pleased Victor. I glanced at Saxon, and his small smile said he was proud of me too.

"What's the course of action now, Sir?" Saxon asked, looking up at his Dominate.

"Well, Alpha Mashkov wasn't happy that there wasn't a majority vote. So he will call another Council Meeting within the next six months" Victor told us.

"And what happens then, Sir?" I questioned.

"Then, Chelsea, I will challenge him for Alpha. And our war will begin".

Mate Claim

Second Volume in Blood Ties Series

Coming Soon

Victor Henderson knew that becoming Alpha would not be easy, but he didn't realise just how hard it would become – when the Alpha refuses to let his position without a fight.

Chelsea is trying to help Victor get into power, but with the Pack being attacked from every angle she doesn't know what to do. And when her own Pack members start turning up dead, she realises this is war they were all dreading.

Can Chelsea help overthrow the Alpha, keep her relationship with Saxon and find the Wolf who is setting Forced Turns on her?

Printed in Great Britain
by Amazon.co.uk, Ltd.,
Marston Gate.